The Heritage of Literature Series

SECTION A NO. 67

THIRTEEN SHORT STORIES

IN ONE MOMENT SHE WAS BESIDE THE SHRIEKING WOMAN

Thirteen Short Stories

HARRY BELL, O.B.E., M.A.

LONGMANS

LONGMANS, GREEN AND CO LTD
48 Grosvenor Street, London W.1

Associated companies, branches and representatives
throughout the world

First published 1957
Second impression 1958
Third impression 1960
Fourth impression 1962
Fifth impression 1963

PRINTED IN GREAT BRITAIN BY
NEILL AND CO LTD EDINBURGH

ACKNOWLEDGMENTS

WE are indebted to the following for permission to reproduce copyright material:

Mr E. C. Bentley for "The Sweet Shot," from *Trent Intervenes*; Messrs Jonathan Cape Ltd., for "Fear," from *Day's End* by H. E. Bates and "The Conger Eel," from *The Short Stories of Liam O'Flaherty*; Messrs Doubleday & Company Inc., for "The Cop and the Anthem," from *The Four Million*, by O. Henry, copyright 1904 by Doubleday & Company Inc.; Mr C. S. Forester, for "The Cargo of Rice," from *Mr Midshipman Hornblower*; Messrs Wm. Heinemann Ltd., for "Quality," from *Caravan*, by John Galsworthy; Messrs John Lane, The Bodley Head Ltd., for "The Stalled Ox," from *The Complete Short Stories of Saki*; Mr Somerset Maugham, Messrs Wm. Heinemann Ltd., and Messrs Doubleday & Company Inc., for "The Luncheon," from *Cosmopolitans*; The Society of Authors and Mr J. Middleton Murry, O.B.E., for *The Voyage*, by Katherine Mansfield; The Tweedsmuir Trustees and Messrs Hodder & Stoughton Ltd., for "The Loathly Opposite," from *The Runagates Club*, by John Buchan; Mrs Norah Walrond, for *The Blue Bead*; The Executors of the late H. G. Wells, for "The Diamond Maker," from *The Stolen Bacillus*; and Mr Iolo Williams, for *The Man Who Stole the Pelican*.

CONTENTS

INTRODUCTION

THE short story has reached an interesting stage in its development. Behind it lies a long history but in the last century or even half-century it has shown the greatest activity, widening its range and increasing its appeal. No doubt this appeal is due in part to the rush of modern life, for some people are unwilling to give their time to leisurely and spacious treatment in a story and ask for something short and snappy. This the short story can supply. With a swift brief stroke it can produce its effect and still leave us without any feeling of incompleteness and inadequacy. In additon a number of modern writers of the first rank, Stevenson, Kipling, Conrad, Wells, Galsworthy and Bates have turned to the short story and used it as a medium capable of the greatest artistry. A rich variety of short stories has resulted.

Engaged as it is in seeking out new directions and new possibilities, the modern short story evades any rigid definition. No sooner have we fixed neat boundary fences round its limits than some author nimbly slips through into a new field. When in 1840 Edgar Allan Poe laid down the conditions governing the short story as an art form (as distinct from a truncated novel), he was in fact, describing only two types: the mystery story and the story of the uncanny. It is true he is the forerunner of the modern detective story and of the modern scientific fantasy, and his influence can thus be traced on E. C. Bentley's *The Sweet Shot* or H. G. Wells's *The Diamond Maker*. But Poe left many fields unexplored.

Poe's main interest lay in the unusual and the extraordinary. It was to everyday life and ordinary people that Guy de Maupassant turned for his stories, and he found his drama in the streets of Paris and fields of Normandy. He describes the life he saw there as if he were a biologist, drawing firm and clear outlines and dissecting with skill. He seems to stand apart, calm and detached, offering no comments but constructing his plots with consummate skill, the parts fitting together as cunningly as in a watch. His best stories, however, are more than masterly dissections, they are communications of living experience.

Somerset Maugham tells us how before he was eighteen he had read all the best of Maupassant's stories. In the galleries of the Odeon in Paris he pored over his discoveries while the busy attendants left him to read in peace. "It is natural enough," he says, "that when at that age I began writing stories myself, I should unconsciously have chosen these little masterpieces as a model. I might very well have hit upon a worse." This is true, and *The Luncheon* in its deft handling, its unexpected turn, and impersonal attitude is clearly in the tradition of de Maupassant's stories.

Meanwhile the Russian Chekhov was turning from external incidents to the inner workings of the heart. "Why write about a man getting into a submarine," he asks, "and going to the North Pole to reconcile himself to the world, while his beloved at that moment throws herself with a hysterical shriek from the belfry? All this is untrue and does not happen in real life. One must write about simple things: how Peter Semionovitch married Maria Ivanovna. That is all." It is not, of course, all, any more than Poe's view or Maupassant's view is all, but it is very important. It is the addition not merely of a new field but of a whole province to the short story.

To some readers Chekhov's sensitive and romantic study of moods seems merely vague and formless. "Nothing happens," they assert. Certainly these delicate sketches leave more to the reader's own feelings and imagination than some readers are willing to give, for Chekhov's oblique approach aims at suggesting impressions rather than stating conclusions. Katherine Mansfield undoubtedly found Chekhov a stimulus. He stimulated her to develop her own talent and she writes freshly, with the freshness not of a new coat of paint but of the glistening grass after a shower of rain. In *The Voyage* the feeling heart and the seeing eye communicate an experience with such directness that we do not at first observe that there is any artistry there at all.

In the United States, O. Henry carried on the Maupassant tradition finding his stories in the streets and apartment houses of New York, and animating them with his own individual humour and sentiment. He specialized in surprise and his trick of an un-expected twist at the end of the story led to a great deal of imitation not all of it skilful. But *The Cop and the Anthem* is vintage O. Henry.

11

Whatever changes may take place in the short story there is one kind that never fails to please many readers: that is the romantic story of adventure. Few can manage it better than C. S. Forester and his story *A Cargo of Rice* introduces his central character Horatio Hornblower who seems likely to join the immortals. John Buchan too is a skilful narrator of this kind of story and *The Loathly Opposite* is a good example of the story that depends on exciting incident and ingenuous situations to make a rattling good yarn! The best adventure stories illumine character as well as depict action and *The Blue Bead* by the promising young author Norah Burke is an anecdote skilfully narrated, but it is something more and lingers in the memory.

Another kind of story that is always a favourite is the humorous story, provided it is well told and not laboured. The humour of Saki is very different from that of O. Henry and *The Stalled Ox* while thoroughly English is also thoroughly individual in its writing. *The Man who stole the Pelican* by I. A. Williams depends for its humour largely on the ingenuity of its plot and its skilful telling.

John Galsworthy reflects a society and outlook that are passing if not past. The leisure and security of Edwardian England have now an old-world flavour but the seeds of change and conflict are clearly seen in Galsworthy's *Quality*. The time and place of the happenings is very important in some stories, but in others it is of little importance. Animal stories for instance such as Liam O'Flaherty's *The Conger Eel* are timeless. That fine artist H. E. Bates generally uses as a background his native district of England around Northamptonshire, but a story like *Fear* might have taken place anywhere.

The aim of this "baker's dozen" of short stories is to offer as rich an assortment as possible. Short stories are of many types. In the more traditional stories plot and character are strongly marked and always make a ready appeal for we are all interested in other human beings and like to know what happened next. When the story deals less with action than with a mood or atmosphere a much greater demand is made on our attention and on our imagination. If we are to appreciate the inner experience that is being conveyed we must be alert to catch all the overtones and undertones, and this demands effort and close sympathetic reading.

The variety of short stories is almost endless. The story may deal with the fantastic, the thrilling, the romantic, or the ordinary. It may have any subject under the sun, indeed in these days of science fiction, even beyond the sun. It may be tender or tough, delicate or powerful, passionate or restrained. The writing may seem to be little more than a squalid piece of realism or it may reflect the lyric quality of poetry. Whatever it is, if it is to survive at all, the short story must be alive.

Not all these stories will appeal equally to every reader. It is hoped, however, that readers will be prepared to meet each story half-way, making the necessary effort to understand and appreciate and thus to capture the joy of true understanding, for "to miss the joy is to miss all."

DOLLAR.   H. BELL.

THE CARGO OF RICE

THE wolf was in among the sheep. The tossing grey water of the Bay of Biscay was dotted with white sails as far as the eye could see, and although a strong breeze was blowing every vessel was under perilously heavy canvas. Every ship but one was trying to escape; the exception was His Majesty's frigate *Indefatigable*, Captain Sir Edward Pellew. Farther out in the Atlantic, hundreds of miles away, a great battle was being fought, where the ships of the line were thrashing out the question as to whether England or France should wield the weapon of sea power; here in the Bay the convoy which the French ships were intended to escort was exposed to the attack of a ship of prey at liberty to capture any ship she could overhaul. She had come surging up from leeward, cutting off all chance of escape in that direction, and the clumsy merchant ships were forced to beat to windward; they were all filled with the food which revolutionary France (her economy disordered by the convulsion through which she was passing) was awaiting so anxiously, and their crews were all anxious to escape confinement in an English prison. Ship after ship was overhauled; a shot or two, and the newfangled tricolour came fluttering down from the gaff, and a prize-crew was hurriedly sent on board to conduct the captive to an English port while the frigate dashed after fresh prey.

On the quarterdeck of the *Indefatigable* Pellew
fumed over each necessary delay. The convoy,
each ship as close to the wind as she would lie, and
under all the sail she could carry, was slowly scatter-
ing, spreading farther and farther with the passing
minutes, and some of these would find safety in mere
dispersion if any time was wasted. Pellew did not
wait to pick up his boat; at each surrender he
merely ordered away an officer and an armed guard,
and the moment the prize-crew was on its way he
filled his main-topsail again and hurried off after the
next victim. The brig they were pursuing at the
moment was slow to surrender. The long nine-
pounders in the *Indefatigable's* bows bellowed out
more than once; on that heaving sea it was not so
easy to aim accurately and the brig continued on her
course hoping for some miracle to save her.

"Very well" snapped Pellew. "He has asked for
it. Let him have it."

The gunlayers at the bow chasers changed their point
of aim, firing at the ship instead of across her bows.

"Not into the hull, damn it" shouted Pellew—
one shot had struck the brig perilously close to her
waterline. "Cripple her."

The next shot by luck or by judgment was given
better elevation. The slings of the foretopsail yard
were shot away, the reefed sail came down, the yard
hanging lop-sidedly, and the brig came up into
the wind for the *Indefatigable* to heave to close beside
her, her broadside ready to fire into her. Under
that threat her flag came down.

"What brig's that?" shouted Pellew through his
megaphone.

"*Marie Galante* of Bordeaux" translated the officer beside Pellew as the French captain made reply. "Twenty-four days out from New Orleans with rice."

"Rice!" said Pellew. "That'll sell for a pretty penny when we get her home. Two hundred tons, I should say. Twelve of a crew at most. She'll need a prize-crew of four, a midshipman's command."

He looked round him as though for inspiration before giving his next order.

"Mr Hornblower!"

"Sir!"

"Take four men of the cutter's crew and board that brig. Mr Soames will give you our position. Take her into any English port you can make, and report there for orders."

"Aye aye, sir."

Hornblower was at his station at the starboard quarterdeck carronades—which was perhaps how he had caught Pellew's eye—his dirk at his side and a pistol in his belt. It was a moment for fast thinking, for anyone could see Pellew's impatience. With the *Indefatigable* cleared for action, his sea chest would be part of the surgeon's operating table down below, so that there was no chance of getting anything out of it. He would have to leave just as he was. The cutter was even now clawing up to a position on the *Indefatigable*'s quarter, so he ran to the ship's side and hailed her, trying to make his voice sound as big and as manly as he could, and at the word of the lieutenant in command she turned her bows in towards the frigate.

"Here's our latitude and longitude, Mr Horn-blower" said Soames, the master, handing a scrap of paper to him.

"Thank you" said Hornblower, shoving it into his pocket.

He scrambled awkwardly into the mizzen-chains and looked down into the cutter. Ship and boat were pitching together, almost bows on to the sea, and the distance between them looked appallingly great; the bearded seaman standing in the bows could only just reach up to the chains with his long boat-hook. Hornblower hesitated for a long second; he knew he was ungainly and awkward—book learning was of no use when it came to jumping into a boat—but he had to make the leap, for Pellew was fuming behind him and the eyes of the boat's crew and of the whole ship's company were on him. Better to jump and hurt himself, better to jump and make an exhibition of himself, than to delay the ship. Waiting was certain failure, while he still had a choice if he jumped. Perhaps at a word from Pellew the *Indefatigable's* helmsman allowed the ship's head to fall off from the sea a little. A somewhat diagonal wave lifted the *Indefatigable's* stern and then passed on, so that the cutter's bows rose as high as the ship's stern sank a trifle. Hornblower braced himself and leaped. His feet reached the gunwale and he tottered there for one indescribable second. A seaman grabbed the breast of his jacket and he fell forward rather than backward. Not even the stout arm of the seaman, fully extended, could hold him up, and he pitched headforemost, legs in the air, upon the hands on the second thwart. He cannoned onto their bodies, knocking the breath out of his own against their muscular shoulders, and finally struggled into an upright position.

"I'm sorry" he gasped to the men who had broken his fall.

"Never you mind, sir" said the nearest one, a real tarry sailor, tattooed and pigtailed. "You're only a featherweight."

The lieutenant in command was looking at him from the stern-sheets.

"Would you go to the brig, please, sir?" he asked, and the lieutenant bawled an order and the cutter swung round as Hornblower made his way aft.

It was a pleasant surprise not to be received with the broad grins of tolerantly concealed amusement. Boarding a small boat from a big frigate in even a moderate sea was no easy matter; probably every man on board had arrived headfirst at some time or other, and it was not in the tradition of the service, as understood in the *Indefatigable*, to laugh at a man who did his best without shirking.

"Are you taking charge of the brig?" asked the lieutenant.

"Yes, sir. The captain told me to take four of your men."

"They had better be topmen, then" said the lieutenant, casting his eyes aloft at the rigging of the brig. The foretopsail yard was hanging precariously, and the jib halliard had slacked off so that the sail was flapping thunderously in the wind. "Do you know these men, or shall I pick 'em for you?"

"I'd be obliged if you would, sir."

The lieutenant shouted four names, and four men replied.

"Keep 'em away from drink and they'll be all right" said the lieutenant. "Watch the French crew. They'll recapture the ship and have you in a French gaol before you can say 'Jack Robinson' if you don't."

"Aye aye, sir" said Hornblower.

The cutter surged alongside the brig, white water creaming between the two vessels. The tattooed sailor hastily concluded a bargain with another man on his thwart and pocketed a lump of tobacco—the men were leaving their possessions behind just like Hornblower—and sprang for the main-chains, Another man followed him, and they stood and waited while Hornblower with difficulty made his way forward along the plunging boat. He stood, balancing precariously, on the forward thwart. The main-chains of the brig were far lower than the mizzen-chains of the *Indefatigable*, but this time he had to jump upwards. One of the seamen steadied him with an arm on his shoulder.

"Wait for it, sir" he said. "Get ready. Now jump, sir."

Hornblower hurled himself, all arms and legs, like a leaping frog, at the main-chains. His hands reached the shrouds, but his knee slipped off, and the brig, rolling, lowered him thigh deep into the sea as the shrouds slipped through his hands. But the waiting seamen grabbed his wrists and hauled him on board, and two more seamen followed him. He led the way onto the deck.

The first sight to meet his eyes was a man seated on

the hatch cover, his head thrown back, holding to his mouth a bottle, the bottom pointing straight up to the sky. He was one of a large group all sitting round the hatch cover; there were more bottles in evidence; one was passed by one man to another as he looked, and as he approached a roll of the ship brought an empty bottle rolling past his toes to clatter into the scuppers. Another of the group, with white hair blowing in the wind, rose to welcome him, and stood for a moment with waving arms and rolling eyes, bracing himself as though to say something of immense importance and seeking earnestly for the right words to use.

"Goddam English" was what he finally said, and, having said it, he sat down with a bump on the hatch cover and from a seated position proceeded to lie down and compose himself to sleep with his head on his arms.

"They've made the best of their time, sir, by the Holy" said the seaman at Hornblower's elbow.

"Wish we were as happy" said another.

A case still a quarter full of bottles, each elaborately sealed, stood on the deck beside the hatch cover, and the seaman picked out a bottle to look at it curiously. Hornblower did not need to remember the lieutenant's warning; on his shore excursions with press gangs he had already had experience of the British seaman's tendency to drink. His boarding party would be as drunk as the Frenchmen in half an hour if he allowed it. A frightful mental picture of himself drifting in the Bay of Biscay with a disabled ship and a drunken crew rose in his mind and filled him with anxiety.

"Put that down" he ordered.

The urgency of the situation made his seventeen-year-old voice crack like a fourteen-year-old's, and the seaman hesitated, holding the bottle in his hand.

"Put it down, d'ye hear?" said Hornblower, desperate with worry. This was his first independent command; conditions were absolutely novel, and excitement brought out all the passion of his mercurial temperament, while at the same time the more calculating part of his mind told him that if he were not obeyed now he never would be. His pistol was in his belt, and he put his hand on the butt, and it is conceivable that he would have drawn it and used it (if the priming had not got wet, he said to himself bitterly when he thought about the incident later on), but the seaman with one more glance at him put the bottle back into the case. The incident was closed, and it was time for the next step.

"Take these men forrard" he said, giving the obvious order. "Throw 'em into the forecastle."

"Aye aye, sir."

Most of the Frenchmen could still walk, but three were dragged by their collars, while the British herded the others before them.

"Come alongee" said one of the seamen. "Thisa waya."

He evidently believed a Frenchman would understand him better if he spoke like that. The Frenchman who had greeted their arrival now awakened, and, suddenly realizing he was being dragged forward, broke away and turned back to Hornblower.

"I officer" he said, pointing to himself. "I not go wit' zem."

"Take him away!" said Hornblower. In his tense condition he could not stop to debate trifles.

He dragged the case of bottles down to the ship's side and pitched them overboard two at a time—obviously it was wine of some special vintage which the Frenchmen had decided to drink before the English could get their hands on it, but that weighed not at all with Hornblower, for a British seaman could get drunk on vintage claret as easily as upon service rum. The task was finished before the last of the Frenchmen disappeared into the forecastle, and Hornblower had time to look about him. The strong breeze blew confusingly round his ears, and the ceaseless thunder of the flapping jib made it hard to think as he looked at the ruin aloft. Every sail was flat aback, the brig was moving jerkily, gathering sternway for a space before her untended rudder threw her round to spill the wind and bring her up again like a jibbing horse. His mathematical mind had already had plenty of experience with a well-handled ship, with the delicate adjustment between after-sails and head-sails. Here the balance had been disturbed, and Hornblower was at work on the problem of forces acting on plane surfaces when his men came trooping back to him. One thing at least was certain, and that was that the precariously hanging foretopsail yard would tear itself free to do all sorts of unforseeable damage if it were tossed about much more. The ship must be properly hove to, and Hornblower could guess how to set about it, and he formulated the order in his mind just in time to avoid any appearance of hesitation.

"Brace the after yards to larboard" he said.
"Man the braces, men."

They obeyed him, while he himself went gingerly
to the wheel; he had served a few tricks as helmsman, learning his professional duties under Pellew's
orders, but he did not feel happy about it. The
spokes felt foreign to his fingers as he took hold;
he spun the wheel experimentally but timidly. But
it was easy. With the after yards braced round, the
brig rode more comfortably at once, and the spokes
told their own story to his sensitive fingers as the ship
became a thing of logical construction again.
Hornblower's mind completed the solution of the
problem of the effect of the rudder at the same time
as his senses solved it empirically. The wheel could
be safely lashed, he knew, in these conditions, and he
slipped the becket over the spoke and stepped away
from the wheel, with the *Marie Galante* riding
comfortably and taking the seas on her starboard
bow.

The seamen took his competence gratifyingly for
granted, but Hornblower, looking at the tangle on
the foremast, had not the remotest idea of how to
deal with the next problem. He was not even sure
about what was wrong. But the hands under his
orders were seamen of vast experience, who must
have dealt with similar emergencies a score of times.
The first—indeed the only—thing to do was to
delegate his responsibility.

"Who's the oldest seaman among you?" he
demanded—his determination not to quaver made
him curt.

"Matthews, sir" said someone at length, indicating

with his thumb the pigtailed and tattooed seaman upon whom he had fallen in the cutter.

"Very well, then. I'll rate you petty officer, Matthews. Get to work at once and clear that raffle away forrard. I'll be busy here aft."

It was a nervous moment for Hornblower, but Matthews put his knuckles to his forehead.

"Aye aye, sir" he said, quite as a matter of course.

"Get that jib in first, before it flogs itself to pieces" said Hornblower, greatly emboldened.

"Aye aye, sir."

"Carry on, then."

The seaman turned to go forward, and Hornblower walked aft. He took the telescope from its becket on the poop, and swept the horizon. There were a few sails in sight; the nearest ones he could recognize as prizes, which, with all sail set that they could carry, were heading for England as fast as they could go. Far away to windward he could see the *Indefatigable's* topsails as she clawed after the rest of the convoy—she had already overhauled and captured all the slower and less weatherly vessels, so that each succeeding chase would be longer. Soon he would be alone on this wide sea, three hundred miles from England. Three hundred miles—two days with a fair wind; but how long if the wind turned foul?

He replaced the telescope; the men were already hard at work forward, so he went below and looked round the neat cabins of the officers; two single ones for the captain and the mate, presumably, and a double one for the bo'sun and the cook or the carpenter. He found the lazarette, identifying it by the miscellaneous stores within it; the door was swinging to and fro with a bunch of keys dangling. The French captain, faced with the loss of all he possessed, had not even troubled to lock the door again after taking out the case of wine. Hornblower locked the door and put the keys in his pocket, and felt suddenly lonely—his first experience of the loneliness of the man in command at sea. He went on deck again, and at sight of him Matthews hurried aft and knuckled his forehead.

"Beg pardon, sir, but we'll have to use the jeers to sling that yard again."

"Very good."

"We'll need more hands than we have, sir. Can I put some o' they Frenchies to work?"

"If you think you can. If any of them are sober enough."

"I think I can, sir. Drunk or sober."

"Very good."

It was at that moment that Hornblower remembered with bitter self-reproach that the priming of his pistol was probably wet, and he had not scorn enough for himself at having put his trust in a pistol without re-priming after evolutions in a small boat. While Matthews went forward he dashed below again. There was a case of pistols which he remembered having seen in the captain's cabin, with a powder flask and bullet bag hanging beside it. He loaded both weapons and reprimed his own, and came on deck again with three pistols in his belt just as his men appeared from the forecastle herding half a dozen Frenchmen. He posed himself in the poop, straddling with his hands behind his back, trying to adopt an air of magnificent indifference and understanding. With the jeers taking the weight of yard and sail, an hour's hard work resulted in the yard being slung again and the sail reset.

When the work was advancing towards completion, Hornblower came to himself again to remember that in a few minutes he would have to set a course, and he dashed below again to set out the chart and the dividers and parallel rulers. From his pocket he extracted the crumpled scrap of paper with his position on it—he had thrust it in there so carelessly a little while back, at a time when the immediate problem before him was to transfer himself from the *Indefatigable* to the cutter. It made him unhappy to think how cavalierly he had treated that scrap of paper then; he began to feel that life in the Navy, although it seemed to move from one crisis to another, was really one continuous crisis, that even while dealing with one emergency it was necessary to be making plans to deal with the next. He bent over the chart, plotted his position, and laid off his course. It was a queer uncomfortable feeling to think that what had up to this moment been an academic exercise conducted under the reassuring supervision of Mr Soames was now something on which hinged his life and his reputation. He checked his working, decided on his course, and wrote it down on a scrap of paper for fear he should forget it.

So when the foretopsail yard was re-slung, and the prisoners herded back into the forecastle, and Matthews looked to him for further orders, he was ready.

"We'll square away" he said. "Matthews, send a man to the wheel."

He himself gave a hand at the braces; the wind had moderated and he felt his men could handle the brig under her present sail.

"What course, sir?" asked the man at the wheel, and Hornblower dived into his pocket for his scrap of paper.

"Nor'-east by north" he said, reading it out.

"Nor'-east by north, sir" said the helmsman; and the *Marie Galante*, running free, set her course for England.

Night was closing in by now, and all round the circle of the horizon there was not a sail in sight. There must be plenty of ships just over the horizon, he knew, but that did not do much to ease his feeling of loneliness as darkness came on. There was so much to do, so much to bear in mind, and all the responsibility lay on his unaccustomed shoulders. The prisoners had to be battened down in the forecastle, a watch had to be set—there was even the trivial matter of hunting up flint and steel to light the binnacle lamp. A hand forward as a lookout, who could also keep an eye on the prisoners below; a hand aft at the wheel. Two hands snatching some sleep—knowing that to get in any sail would be an all-hands job—a hasty meal of water from the scuttle-butt and of biscuit from the cabin stores in the lazarette—a constant eye to be kept on the weather. Hornblower paced the deck in the darkness.

"Why don't you get some sleep, sir?" asked the man at the wheel.

"I will, later on, Hunter" said Hornblower, trying not to allow his tone to reveal the fact that such a thing had never occurred to him.

He knew it was sensible advice, and he actually tried to follow it, retiring below to fling himself down on the captain's cot; but of course he could not sleep. When he heard the lookout bawling down the companionway to rouse the other two hands to relieve the watch (they were asleep in the next cabin to him) he could not prevent himself from getting up again and coming on deck to see that all was well. With Matthews in charge he felt he should not be anxious, and he drove himself below again, but he had hardly fallen onto the cot again when a new thought brought him to his feet again, his skin cold with anxiety, and a prodigious self-contempt vying with anxiety for first place in his emotions. He rushed on deck and walked forward to where Matthews was squatting by the knightheads.

"Nothing has been done to see if the brig is taking in any water" he said—he had hurriedly worked out the wording of that sentence during his walk forward, so as to cast no aspersion on Matthews and yet at the same time, for the sake of discipline, attributing no blame to himself.

"That's so, sir" said Matthews.

"One of those shots fired by the *Indefatigable* hulled her" went on Hornblower. "What damage did it do?"

"I don't rightly know, sir" said Matthews. "I was in the cutter at the time."

"We must look as soon as it's light" said Hornblower. "And we'd better sound the well now."

Those were brave words; during his rapid course in seamanship aboard the *Indefatigable* Hornblower had had a little instruction everywhere, working under the orders of every head of department in rotation. Once he had been with the carpenter when he sounded the well—whether he could find the well in this ship and sound it he did not know.

"Aye aye, sir" said Matthews, without hesitation, and strolled aft to the pump. "You'll need a light, sir. I'll get one."

When he came back with the lantern he shone it on the coiled sounding line hanging beside the pump, so that Hornblower recognized it at once. He lifted it down, inserted the three-foot weighted rod into the aperture of the well, and then remembered in time to take it out again and make sure it was dry. Then he let it drop, paying out the line until he felt the rod strike the ship's bottom with a satisfactory thud. He hauled out the line again, and Matthews held the lantern as Hornblower with some trepidation brought out the timber to examine it.

"Not a drop, sir!" said Matthews. "Dry as yesterday's pannikin."

Hornblower was agreeably surprised. Any ship he had ever heard of leaked to a certain extent; even in the well-found *Indefatigable* pumping had been necessary every day. He did not know whether this dryness was a remarkable phenomenon or a very remarkable one. He wanted to be both non-committal and imperturbable.

"H'm" was the comment he eventually produced. "Very good, Matthews. Coil that line again."

The knowledge that the *Marie Galante* was making no water at all might have encouraged him to sleep, if the wind had not chosen to veer steadily and strengthen itself somewhat soon after he retired again. It was Matthews who came down and pounded on his door with the unwelcome news.

"We can't keep the course you set much longer, sir" concluded Matthews. "And the wind's coming gusty-like."

"Very good, I'll be up. Call all hands" said Hornblower, with a testiness that might have been the result of a sudden awakening if it had not really disguised his inner quaverings.

With such a small crew he dared not run the slightest risk of being taken by surprise by the weather. Nothing could be done in a hurry, as he soon found. He had to take the wheel while his four hands laboured at reefing topsails and snugging the brig down; the task took half the night, and by the time it was finished it was quite plain that with the wind veering northerly the *Marie Galante* could not steer north-east by north any longer. Hornblower gave up the wheel and went below to the chart, but what he saw there only confirmed the pessimistic decision he had already reached by mental calculation. As close to the wind as they could lie on this tack they could not weather Ushant. Short-handed as he was he did not dare continue in the hope that the wind might back; all his reading and all his instruction had warned him of the terrors of a lee shore. There was nothing for it but to go about; he returned to the deck with a heavy heart.

"All hands wear ship" he said, trying to bellow the

31

order in the manner of Mr Bolton, the third lieutenant of the *Indefatigable*.

They brought the brig safely round, and she took up her new course, close hauled on the starboard tack. Now she was heading away from the dangerous shores of France, without a doubt, but she was heading nearly as directly away from the friendly shores of England—gone was all hope of an easy two days' run to England; gone was any hope of sleep that night for Hornblower.

During the year before he joined the Navy Hornblower had attended classes given by a penniless French émigré in French, music, and dancing. Early enough the wretched émigré had found that Hornblower had no ear for music whatever, which made it almost impossible to teach him to dance, and so he had endeavoured to earn his fee by concentrating on French. A good deal of what he had taught Hornblower had found a permanent resting place in Hornblower's tenacious memory. He had never thought it would be of much use to him, but he discovered the contrary when the French captain at dawn insisted on an interview with him. The Frenchman had a little English, but it was a pleasant surprise to Hornblower to find that they actually could get along better in French, as soon as he could fight down his shyness sufficiently to produce the halting words.

The captain drank thirstily from the scuttlebutt; his cheeks were of course unshaven and he wore a bleary look after twelve hours in a crowded forecastle, where he had been battened down three parts drunk.

"My men are hungry" said the captain; he did not look hungry himself.

"Mine also" said Hornblower. "I also."

It was natural when one spoke French to gesticulate, to indicate his men with a wave of the hand and himself with a tap on the chest.

"I have a cook" said the captain.

It took some time to arrange the terms of a truce. The Frenchmen were to be allowed on deck, the cook was to provide food for everyone on board, and while these amenities were permitted, until noon, the French would make no attempt to take the ship.

"Good" said the captain at length; and when Hornblower had given the necessary orders permitting the release of the crew he shouted for the cook and entered into an urgent discussion regarding dinner. Soon smoke was issuing satisfactorily from the galley chimney.

Then the captain looked up at the grey sky, at the close reefed topsails, and glanced into the binnacle at the compass.

"A foul wind for England" he remarked.

"Yes" said Hornblower shortly. He did not want this Frenchman to guess at his trepidation and bitterness.

The captain seemed to be feeling the motion of the brig under his feet with attention.

"She rides a little heavily, does she not?" he said.

"Perhaps" said Hornblower. He was not familiar with the *Marie Galante*, nor with ships at all, and he had no opinion on the subject, but he was not going to reveal his ignorance.

"Does she leak?" asked the captain.

"There is no water in her" said Hornblower.

"Ah!" said the captain. "But you would find none in the well. We are carrying a cargo of rice, you must remember."

"Yes" said Hornblower.

He found it very hard at that moment to remain outwardly unperturbed, as his mind grasped the implications of what was being said to him. Rice would absorb every drop of water taken in by the ship, so that no leak would be apparent on sounding the well—and yet every drop of water taken in would deprive her of that much buoyancy, all the same.

"One shot from your cursed frigate struck us in the hull" said the captain. "Of course you have investigated the damage?"

"Of course" said Hornblower, lying bravely.

But as soon as he could he had a private conversation with Matthews on the point, and Matthews instantly looked grave.

"Where did the shot hit her, sir?" he asked.

"Somewhere on the port side, forrard, I should judge."

He and Matthews craned their necks over the ship's side.

"Can't see nothin', sir" said Matthews. "Lower me over the side in a bowline and I'll see what I can find, sir."

Hornblower was about to agree and then changed his mind.

"I'll go over the side myself" he said.

He could not analyse the motives which impelled him to say that. Partly he wanted to see things

34

with his own eyes; partly he was influenced by the doctrine that he should never give an order he was not prepared to carry out himself—but mostly it must have been the desire to impose a penance on himself for his negligence.

Matthews and Carson put a bowline round him and lowered him over. He found himself dangling against the ship's side, with the sea bubbling just below him; as the ship pitched the sea came up to meet him, and he was wet to the waist in the first five seconds; and as the ship rolled he was alternately swung away from the side and bumped against it. The men with the line walked steadily aft, giving him the chance to examine the whole side of the brig above water, and there was not a shot hole to be seen. He said as much to Matthews when they hauled him on deck.

"Then it's below the waterline, sir" said Matthews, saying just what was in Hornblower's mind. "You're sure the shot hit her, sir?"

"Yes, I'm sure" snapped Hornblower.

Lack of sleep and worry and a sense of guilt were all shortening his temper, and he had to speak sharply or break down in tears. But he had already decided on the next move—he had made up his mind about that while they were hauling him up.

"We'll heave her to on the other tack and try again" he said.

On the other tack the ship would incline over to the other side, and the shot-hole, if there was one, would not be so deeply submerged. Hornblower stood with the water dripping from his clothes as they wore the brig round; the wind was keen and

cold, but he was shivering with expectancy rather
than cold. The heeling of the brig laid him much
more definitely against the side, and they lowered
him until his legs were scraping over the marine
growths which she carried there between wind and
water. They then walked aft with him, dragging
him along the side of the ship, and just abaft the
foremast he found what he was seeking.

"Avast, there!" he yelled up to the deck, mastering
the sick despair that he felt. The motion of the bowline along the ship ceased. "Lower away! Another
two feet!"

Now he was waist-deep in the water, and when the
brig swayed the water closed briefly over his head,
like a momentary death. Here it was, two feet
below the waterline even with the brig hove to on
this tack—a splintered, jagged hole, square rather
than round, and a foot across. As the sea boiled
round him Hornblower even fancied he could hear it
bubbling into the ship, but that might be pure fancy.

He hailed the deck for them to haul him up again,
and they stood eagerly listening for what he had to say.

"Two feet below the waterline, sir?" said
Matthews. "She was close hauled and heeling
right over, of course, when we hit her. But her
bows must have lifted just as we fired. And of
course she's lower in the water now."

That was the point. Whatever they did now,
however much they heeled her, that hole would be
under water. And on the other tack it would be
far under water, with much additional pressure;
yet on the present tack they were headed for France.
And the more water they took in, the lower the brig

would settle, and the greater would be the pressure forcing water in through the hole. Something must be done to plug the leak, and Hornblower's reading of the manuals of seamanship told him what it was.

"We must fother a sail and get it over that hole" he announced. "Call those Frenchmen over."

To fother a sail was to make something like a vast hairy doormat out of it, by threading innumerable lengths of half-unravelled line through it. When this was done the sail would be lowered below the ship's bottom and placed against the hole. The inward pressure would then force the hairy mass so tightly against the hole that the entrance of water would be made at least much more difficult.

The Frenchmen were not quick to help in the task; it was no longer their ship, and they were heading for an English prison, so that even with their lives at stake they were somewhat apathetic. It took time to get out a new topgallant sail—Hornblower felt that the stouter the canvas the better—and set a party to work cutting lengths of line, threading them through, and unravelling them. The French captain looked at them squatting on the deck all at work.

"Five years I spent in a prison hulk in Portsmouth during the last war" he said. "Five years."

"Yes" said Hornblower.

He might have felt sympathy, but he was not only preoccupied with his own problems but he was numb with cold. He not only had every intention if possible of escorting the French captain to England and to prison again but he also at that very moment intended to go below and appropriate some of his spare clothing.

Down below it seemed to Hornblower as if the noises all about him—the creaks and groans of a wooden ship at sea—were more pronounced than usual. The brig was riding easily enough hove-to, and yet the bulkheads down below were cracking and creaking as if the brig were racking herself to pieces in a storm. He dismissed the notion as a product of his over-stimulated imagination, but by the time he had towelled himself into something like warmth and put on the captain's best suit it recurred to him; the brig was groaning as if in stress.

He came on deck again to see how the working party was progressing. He had hardly been on deck two minutes when one of the Frenchmen, reaching back for another length of line, stopped in his movement to stare at the deck. He picked at a deck seam, looked up and caught Hornblower's eye, and called to him. Hornblower made no pretence of understanding the words; the gestures explained themselves. The deck seam was opening a little; the pitch was bulging out of it. Hornblower looked at the phenomenon without understanding it—only a foot or two of the seam was open, and the rest of the deck seemed solid enough. No! Now that his attention was called to it, and he looked further, there were one or two other places in the deck where the pitch had risen in ridges from out of the seams. It was something beyond his limited experience, even beyond his extensive reading. But the French captain was at his side staring at the deck too.

"My God!" he said. "The rice! The rice!"

The French word 'riz' that he used was unknown

to Hornblower, but he stamped his foot on the deck and pointed down through it.

"The cargo!" he said in explanation. "It—it grows bigger."

Matthews was with them now, and without knowing a word of French he understood.

"Didn't I hear this brig was full of rice, sir?" he asked.

"Yes."

"That's it then. The water's got into it and it's swelling." So it would. Dry rice soaked in water would double or treble its volume. The cargo was swelling and bursting the seams of the ship open. Hornblower remembered the unnatural creaks and groans below. It was a black moment; he looked round at the unfriendly sea for inspiration and support, and found neither. Several seconds passed before he was ready to speak, and ready to maintain the dignity of a naval officer in face of difficulties.

"The sooner we get that sail over that hole the better, then" he said. It was too much to be expected that his voice should sound quite natural. "Hurry those Frenchmen up."

He turned to pace the deck, so as to allow his feelings to subside and to set his thoughts running in an orderly fashion again, but the French captain was at his elbow, voluble as a Job's comforter.

"I said I thought the ship was riding heavily" he said. "She is lower in the water."

"Go to the devil" said Hornblower, in English— he could not think up the French for that phrase.

Even as he stood he felt a sudden sharp shock beneath his feet, as if someone had hit the deck

39

underneath them with a mallet. The ship was springing apart bit by bit.

"Hurry with that sail!" he yelled, turning back to the working party, and then was angry with himself because the tone of his voice must have betrayed undignified agitation.

At last an area of five feet square of the sail was fothered, lines were rove through the grommets, and the working party hurried forward to work the sail under the brig and drag it aft to the hole. Hornblower was taking off his clothes, not out of regard for the captain's property but so as to keep them dry for himself.

"I'll go over and see that it's in place" he said. "Matthews, get a bowline ready for me."

Naked and wet, it seemed to him as if the wind blew clear through him; rubbing against the ship's side as she rolled he lost a good deal of skin, and the waves passing down the ship smacked at him with a boisterous lack of consideration. But he saw the fothered sail placed against the hole, and with intense satisfaction he saw the hairy mass suck into position, dimpling over the hole to form a deep hollow so that he could be sure that the hole was plugged solid. They hauled him up again when he hailed, and awaited his orders; he stood naked, stupid with cold and fatigue and lack of sleep, struggling to form his next decision.

"Lay her on the starboard tack" he said at length.

If the brig were going to sink, it hardly mattered if it were one hundred or two hundred miles from the French coast; if she were to stay afloat he wanted to be well clear of that lee shore and the chance of recapture. The shot hole with its fothered sail would be deeper under water to increase the risk, but it seemed to be the best chance. The French captain saw them making preparations to wear the brig round, and turned upon Hornblower with voluble protests. With this wind they could make Bordeaux easily on the other tack. Hornblower was risking all their lives, he said. Into Hornblower's numb mind crept, uninvited, the translation of something he had previously wanted to say. He could use it now.

"Allez au diable" he snapped, as he put the Frenchman's stout woollen shirt on over his head.

When his head emerged the Frenchman was still protesting volubly, so violently indeed that a new doubt came into Hornblower's mind. A word to Matthews sent him round the French prisoners to search for weapons. There was nothing to be found except the sailors' knives, but as a matter of precaution Hornblower had them all impounded, and when he had dressed he went to special trouble with his three pistols, drawing the charges from them and reloading and repriming afresh. Three pistols in his belt looked piratical, as though he were still young enough to be playing imaginative games, but Hornblower felt in his bones that there might be a time when the Frenchmen might try to rise against their captors, and three pistols would not be too many against twelve desperate men who had makeshift weapons ready to hand, belaying pins and the like.

Matthews was awaiting him with a long face.

"Sir" he said "begging your pardon, but I don't

like the looks of it. Straight, I don't. I don't like the feel of her. She's settlin' down and she's openin' up, I'm certain sure. Beg your pardon, sir, for saying so."

Down below Hornblower had heard the fabric of the ship continuing to crack and complain; up here the deck seams were gaping more widely. There was a very likely explanation; the swelling of the rice must have forced open the ship's seams below water, so that plugging the shot-hole would have only eliminated what would be by now only a minor leak. Water must still be pouring in, the cargo still swelling, opening up the ship like an overblown flower. Ships were built to withstand blows from without, and there was nothing about their construction to resist an outward pressure. Wider and wider would gape the seams, and faster and faster the sea would gain access to the cargo.

"Look'e there, sir!" said Matthews suddenly.

In the broad light of day a small grey shape was hurrying along the weather scuppers; another one followed it and another after that. Rats! Something convulsive must be going on down below to bring them on deck in daytime, from out of their comfortable nests among the unlimited food of the cargo. The pressure must be enormous. Hornblower felt another small shock beneath his feet at that moment, as something further parted beneath them. But there was one more card to play, one last line of defence that he could think of.

"I'll jettison the cargo" said Hornblower. He had never uttered that word in his life, but he had read it. "Get the prisoners and we'll start."

The battened-down hatch cover was domed upwards curiously and significantly; as the wedges were knocked out one plank tore loose at one end with a crash, pointing diagonally upwards, and as the working party lifted off the cover a brown form followed it upwards—a bag of rice, forced out by the underlying pressure until it jammed in the hatchway.

"Tail onto those tackles and sway it up" said Hornblower.

Bag by bag the rice was hauled up from the hold; sometimes the bags split, allowing a torrent of rice to pour onto the deck, but that did not matter. Another section of the working party swept rice and bags to the lee side and into the ever-hungry sea. After the first three bags the difficulties increased, for the cargo was so tightly jammed below that it called for enormous force to tear each bag out of its position. Two men had to go down the hatchway to pry the bags loose and adjust the slings. There was a momentary hesitation on the part of the two Frenchmen to whom Hornblower pointed—the bags might not all be jammed and the hold of a tossing ship was a dangerous place wherein a roll might bury them alive—but Hornblower had no thought at that moment for other people's human fears. He scowled at the brief check and they hastened to lower themselves down the hatchway. The labour was enormous as it went on hour after hour; the men at the tackles were dripping with sweat and drooping with fatigue, but they had to relieve periodically the men below, for the bags had jammed themselves in tiers, pressed hard against the ship's bottom below and the deck beams above, and when the bags immediately below the hatchway had been swayed up the surrounding ones had to be pried loose, out of each tier. Then when a small clearance had been made in the neighbourhood of the hatchway, and they were getting deeper down into the hold, they made the inevitable discovery. The lower tiers of bags had been wetted, their contents had swelled, and the bags had burst. The lower half of the hold was packed solid with damp rice which could only be got out with shovels and a hoist. The still intact bags of the upper tiers, farther away from the hatchway, were still jammed tight, calling for much labour to free them and to manhandle them under the hatchway to be hoisted out.

Hornblower, facing the problem, was distracted by a touch on his elbow when Matthews came up to speak to him.

"It ain't no go, sir" said Matthews. "She's lower in the water an' settlin' fast."

Hornblower walked to the ship's side with him and looked over. There could be no doubt about it. He had been over the side himself and could remember the height of the waterline, and he had for a more exact guide the level of the fothered sail under the ship's bottom. The brig was a full six inches lower in the water—and this after fifty tons of rice at least had been hoisted out and flung over the side. The brig must be leaking like a basket, with water pouring in through the gaping seams to be sucked up immediately by the thirsty rice.

Hornblower's left hand was hurting him, and he looked down to discover that he was gripping the rail with it so tightly as to cause him pain, without knowing he was doing so. He released his grip and looked about him, at the afternoon sun, at the tossing sea. He did not want to give in and admit defeat. The French captain came up to him.

"This is folly" he said. "Madness, sir. My men are overcome by fatigue."

Over by the hatchway, Hornblower saw, Hunter was driving the French seamen to their work with a rope's end, which he was using furiously. There was not much more work to be got out of the Frenchmen; and at that moment the *Marie Galante* rose heavily to a wave and wallowed down the further side. Even his inexperience could detect the sluggishness and ominous deadness of her movements. The brig had not much longer to float, and there was a good deal to do.

"I shall make preparations for abandoning the ship, Matthews" he said.

He poked his chin upwards as he spoke; he would not allow either a Frenchman or a seaman to guess at his despair.

"Aye aye, sir" said Matthews.

The *Marie Galante* carried a boat on chocks abaft the mainmast; at Matthews' summons the men abandoned their work on the cargo and hurried to the business of putting food and water in her.

"Beggin' your pardon, sir" said Hunter aside to Hornblower, "but you ought to see you have warm clothes, sir. I been in an open boat ten days once, sir."

"Thank you, Hunter" said Hornblower.

There was much to think of. Navigating instruments, charts, compass—would he be able to get a good observation with his sextant in a tossing little boat? Common prudence dictated that they should have all the food and water with them that the boat could carry; but—Hornblower eyed the wretched craft dubiously—seventeen men would fill it to overflowing anyway. He would have to leave much to the judgment of the French captain and of Matthews.

The tackles were manned and the boat was swayed up from the chocks and lowered into the water in the tiny lee afforded on the lee quarter. The *Marie Galante* put her nose into a wave, refusing to rise to it; green water came over the starboard bow and poured aft along the deck before a sullen wallow on the part of the brig sent it into the scuppers. There was not much time to spare—a rending crash from below told that the cargo was still swelling and forcing the bulkheads. There was a panic among the Frenchmen, who began to tumble down into the boat with loud cries. The French captain took one look at Hornblower and then followed them; two of the British seamen were already over the side fending off the boat.

"Go along" said Hornblower to Matthews and Carson, who still lingered. He was the captain; it was his place to leave the ship last.

So waterlogged was the brig now that it was not at all difficult to step down into the boat from the deck; the British seamen were in the sternsheets and made room for him.

"Take the tiller, Matthews" said Hornblower; he did not feel he was competent to handle that overloaded boat. "Shove off, there!"

46

The boat and the brig parted company; the *Marie Galante*, with her helm lashed, poked her nose into the wind and hung there. She had acquired a sudden list, with the starboard side scuppers nearly under water. Another wave broke over her deck, pouring up to the open hatchway. Now she righted herself, her deck nearly level with the sea, and then she sank, on an even keel, the water closing over her, her masts slowly disappearing. For an instant her sails even gleamed under the green water.

"She's gone" said Matthews.

Hornblower watched the disappearance of his first command. The *Marie Galante* had been entrusted to him to bring into port, and he had failed, failed on his first independent mission. He looked very hard at the setting sun, hoping no one would notice the tears that were filling his eyes.

C. S. FORESTER—*Mr Midshipman Hornblower.*

THE CONGER EEL

He was eight feet long. At the centre of his back
he was two feet in circumference. Slipping sinu-
ously along the bottom of the sea at a gigantic pace,
his black, mysterious body glistened and twirled
like a wisp in a foaming cataract. His little eyes,
stationed wide apart in his flat-boned, broad skull,
searched the ocean for food. He coursed ravenously
for miles along the base of the range of cliffs. He
searched fruitlessly, except for three baby pollocks
which he swallowed in one mouthful without
arresting his progress. He was very hungry.

Then he turned by a sharp promontory and
entered a cliff-bound harbour where the sea was
dark and silent, shaded by the concave cliffs.
Savagely he looked ahead into the dark waters.
Then instantaneously he flicked his tail, rippling
his body like a twisted screw, and shot forward. His
long, thin, single whisker, hanging from his lower
snout like a label tag, jerked back under his belly.
His glassy eyes rested ferociously on minute white
spots that scurried about in the sea a long distance
ahead. The conger eel had sighted his prey. There
was a school of mackerel a mile away.

He came upon them headlong, in a flash. He rose
out of the deep from beneath their white bellies,
and gripped one mackerel in his wide-open jaws ere
his snout met the surface. Then, as if in a swoon,

his body went limp, and tumbling over and over, convulsing like a crushed worm, he sank lower and lower until at last he had swallowed the fish. Then immediately he straightened out and flicked his tail, ready to pursue his prey afresh.

The school of mackerel, when the dread monster had appeared among them, were swimming just beneath the surface of the sea. When the eel rushed up they had hurled themselves clean out of the water with the sound of innumerable grains of sand being shaken in an immense sieve. The thousand blue and white bodies flashed and shimmered in the sun for three moments, and then they disappeared, leaving a large patch of the dark water convulsing turbulently. Ten thousand little fins cut the surface of the sea as the mackerel set off in headlong flight. Their white bellies were no longer visible. They plunged down into the depths of the sea, where their blue-black sides and backs, the colour of the sea, hid them from their enemy. The eel surged about in immense figures of eight; but he had lost them.

Half hungry, half satisfied, he roamed about for half an hour, a demented giant of the deep, travelling restlessly at an incredible speed. Then at last his little eyes again sighted his prey. Little white spots again hung like faded drops of brine in the sea ahead of him. He rushed thither. He opened his jaws as the spots assumed shape, and they loomed up close to his eyes. But just as he attempted to gobble the nearest one, he felt a savage impact. Then something hard and yet intangible pressed against his head and then down along his back. He leaped

and turned somersault. The hard, gripping
material completely enveloped him. He was in a
net. While on all sides of him mackerel wriggled
gasping in the meshes.

The eel paused for two seconds amazed and
terrified. Then all around him he saw a web of
black strands hanging miraculously in the water,
everywhere, while mackerel with heaving gills stood
rigid in the web, some with their tails and heads
both caught and their bodies curved in an arch,
others encompassed many times in the uneven folds,
others girdled firmly below the gills with a single
black thread. Glittering, they eddied back and
forth with the stream of the sea, a mass of fish being
strangled in the deep.

Then the eel began to struggle fiercely to escape.
He hurtled hither and thither, swinging his long slippery body backwards and forwards, ripping with his
snout, surging forward suddenly at full speed,
churning the water. He ripped and tore the net,
cutting great long gashes in it. But the more he cut
and ripped the more deeply enmeshed did he become. He did not release himself, but he released
some of the mackerel. They fell from the torn
meshes, stiff and crippled, downwards, sinking like
dead things. Then suddenly one after another they
seemed to wake from sleep, shook their tails, and
darted away, while the giant eel was gathering coil
upon coil of the net about his slippery body. Then,
at last, exhausted and half strangled, he lay still,
heaving.

Presently he felt himself being hauled up in the net.
The net crowded around him more, so that the

little gleaming mackerel, imprisoned with him, rubbed his sides and lay soft and flabby against him, all hauled up in the net with him. He lay still. He reached the surface and gasped, but he made no movement. Then he was hauled heavily into a boat, and fell with a thud into the bottom.

The two fishermen in the boat began to curse violently when they saw the monstrous eel that had torn their net and ruined their catch of mackerel. The old man on the oars in the bow called out: "Free him and kill him." The young man who was hauling in the net looked in terror at the slippery monster that lay between his feet, with its little eyes looking up cunningly, as if it were human. He almost trembled as he picked up the net and began to undo the coils. "Slash it with your knife", yelled the old man, "before he does more harm". The young man picked up his knife from the gunwale where it was stuck, and cut the net, freeing the eel. The eel, with a sudden and amazing movement, glided up the bottom of the boat, so that he stretched full length.

Then he doubled back, rocking the boat as he beat the sides with his whirling tail, his belly flopping in the water that lay in the bottom. The two men screamed, both crying: "Kill him, or he'll drown us." "Strike him on the nable." They both reached for the short, thick stick that hung from a peg amidships. The young man grabbed it, bent down, and struck at the eel. "Hit him on the nable!" cried the old man; "catch him, catch him, and turn him over."

They both bent down, pawing at the eel, cursing

and panting, while the boat rocked ominously and the huge conger eel glided around and around at an amazing speed. Their hands clawed his sides, slipping over them like skates on ice. They gripped him with their knees, they stood on him, they tried to lie on him, but in their confusion they could not catch him.

Then at last the young man lifted him in his arms, holding him in the middle, gripping him as if he were trying to crush him to death. He staggered upwards. "Now strike him on the nable!" he yelled to the old man. But suddenly he staggered backwards. The boat rocked. He dropped the eel with an oath, reaching out with his hands to steady himself. The eel's head fell over the canted gunwale. His snout dipped into the sea. With an immense shiver he glided away, straight down, down to the depths, down like an arrow, until he reached the dark, weed-covered rocks at the bottom.

Then stretching out to his full length he coursed in a wide arc to his enormous lair, far away in the silent depths.

LIAM O'FLAHERTY—*The Short Stories of.*

THE SWEET SHOT

"No; I happened to be abroad at the time," Philip Trent said. "I wasn't in the way of seeing the English papers, so until I came here this week I never heard anything about your mystery."

Captain Royden, a small, spare, brown-faced man, was engaged in the delicate—and forbidden—task of taking his automatic telephone instrument to pieces. He now suspended his labours and reached for the tobacco-jar. The large window of his office in the Kempshill clubhouse looked down upon the eighteenth green of that delectable golf course, and his eye roved over the whinclad slopes beyond as he called on his recollection.

"Well, if you call it a mystery," he said as he filled a pipe. "Some people do, because they like mysteries, I suppose. For instance, Colin Hunt, the man you're staying with, calls it that. Others won't have it, and say there was a perfectly natural explanation. I could tell you as much as anybody could about it, I dare say."

"As being secretary here, you mean?"

"Not only that. I was one of the two people who were in at the death, so to speak—or next door to it," Captain Royden said. He limped to the mantel-shelf and took down a silver box embossed on the lid with the crest and mottoes of the Corps of Royal Engineers. "Try one of these cigarettes, Mr Trent.

If you'd like to hear the yarn, I'll give it you. You have heard something about Arthur Freer, I suppose?"

"Hardly anything," Trent said. "I just gathered that he wasn't a very popular character."

"No," Captain Royden said with reserve. "Did they tell you he was my brother-in-law? No? Well, now, it happened about four months ago, on a Monday—let me see—yes, the second Monday in May. Freer had a habit of playing nine holes before breakfast. Barring Sundays—he was strict about Sunday—he did it most days, even in the beastliest weather, going round all alone usually, carrying his own clubs, studying every shot as if his life depended on it. That helped to make him the very good player he was. His handicap here was two, and at Undershaw he used to be scratch, I believe.

"At a quarter to eight he'd be on the first tee, and by nine he'd be back at his house—it's only a few minutes from here. That Monday morning he started off as usual—"

"And at the usual time?"

"Just about. He had spent a few minutes in the clubroom blowing up the steward about some trifle. And that was the last time he was seen alive by anybody—near enough to speak of, that is. No one else went off the first tee until a little after nine, when I started round with Browson—he's our local padre; I had been having breakfast with him at the Vicarage. He's got a game leg, like me, so we often play together when he can fit it in.

"We had holed out on the first green, and were walking on to the next tee, when Browson said,

"Great Scot! Look there. Something's happened!"
He pointed down the fairway of the second hole;
and there we could see a man lying sprawled on
the turf, face down and motionless. Now there is
this point about the second hole—the first half of it
is in a dip in the land, just deep enough to be out of
sight from any other point on the course, unless
you're standing right above it—you'll see when you
go round yourself. Well, on the tee, you *are* right
above it; and we saw this man lying. We ran to the
spot.

"It was Freer, as I had known it must be at that
hour. He was dead, lying in a disjointed sort of way
no live man could have lain in. His clothing was
torn to ribbons, and it was singed too. So was his
hair—he used to play bareheaded—and his face
and hands. His bag of clubs was lying a few yards
away, and the brassie, which he had just been using,
was close by the body.

"There wasn't any wound showing, and I had
seen far worse things often enough, but the padre
was looking sickish, so I asked him to go back to the
clubhouse and send for a doctor and the police while
I mounted guard. They weren't long coming, and
after they had done their job the body was taken
away in an ambulance. Well, that's about all I
can tell you at first hand, Mr Trent. If you are
staying with Hunt, you'll have heard about the
inquest and all that, probably."

Trent shook his head. "No," he said. "Colin
was just beginning to tell me, after breakfast this
morning, about Freer having been killed on the
course in some incomprehensible way, when a man

55

came to see him about something. So, as I was
going to apply for a fortnight's run of the course,
I thought I would ask you about the affair."

"All right," Captain Royden said. "I can tell
you about the inquest anyhow—had to be there to
speak my own little piece, about finding the body.
As for what had happened to Freer, the medical
evidence was rather confusing. It was agreed that
he had been killed by some tremendous shock,
which had jolted his whole system to pieces and dis-
located several joints, but had been not quite violent
enough to cause any visible wound. Apart from
that, there was a disagreement. Freer's own
doctor, who saw the body first, declared he must
have been struck by lightning. He said it was true
there hadn't been a thunder-storm, but that there
had been thunder about all that week-end, but that
sometimes lightning did act in that way. But the
police surgeon, Collins, said there would be no such
displacement of the organs from a lightning stroke,
even if it did ever happen that way in our climate,
which he doubted. And he said that if it had been
lightning, it would have struck the steel-headed
clubs; but the clubs lay there in their bag quite
undamaged. Collins thought there must have been
some kind of explosion, though he couldn't suggest
what kind."

Trent shook his head. "I don't suppose that
impressed the court," he said. "All the same, it
may have been all the honest opinion he could give."
He smoked in silence a few moments, while Captain
Royden attended to the troubles of his telephone
instrument with a camel-hair brush. "But surely,"

Trent said at length, "if there had been such an explosion as that, somebody would have heard the sound of it."

"Lots of people would have heard it," Captain Royden answered. "But there you are, you see—nobody notices the sound of explosions just about here. There's the quarry on the other side of the road there, and any time after seven A.M. there's liable to be a noise of blasting."

"A dull, sickening thud?"

"Jolly sickening," Captain Royden said, "for all of us living near by. And so that point wasn't raised. Well, Collins is a very sound man; but, as you say, his evidence didn't really explain the thing, and the other fellow's did, whether it was right or wrong. Besides, the coroner and the jury had heard about a bolt from a clear sky, and the notion appealed to them. Anyhow, they brought it in death from misadventure."

"Which nobody could deny, as the song says," Trent remarked. "And was there no other evidence?"

"Yes, some. But Hunt can tell you about it as well as I can; he was there. I shall have to ask you to excuse me now," Captain Royden said. "I have an appointment in the town. The steward will sign you on for a fortnight, and probably get you a game too, if you want one to-day."

Colin Hunt and his wife, when Trent returned to their house for luncheon, were very willing to complete the tale. The verdict, they declared, was tripe. Dr Collins knew his job, whereas Dr Hoyle was an old footler, and Freer's death had never been reasonably explained.

As for the other evidence, it had, they agreed, been interesting, though it didn't help at all. Freer had been seen after he had played his tee-shot at the second hole, when he was walking down to the bottom of the dip towards the spot where he met his death.

"But according to Royden," Trent said, "that was a place where he couldn't be seen, unless one was right above him."

"Well, this witness *was* right above him," Hunt rejoined. "About one thousand feet above him, so he said. He was an R.A.F. man, piloting a bomber from Bexford Camp, not far from here. He was up doing some sort of exercise, and passed over the course just at that time. He didn't know Freer, but he spotted a man walking down from the second tee, because he was the only living soul visible on the course. Gossett, the other man in the plane, is a temporary member here, and he did know Freer quite well—or as well as anybody cared to know him—but he never saw him. However, the pilot was quite clear that he saw a man just at the time in question, and they took his evidence so as to prove that Freer was absolutely alone just before his death. The only other person who saw Freer was another man who knew him well; used to be a caddy here, and then got a job at the quarry. He was at work on the hillside, and he watched Freer play the first hole and go on to the second—nobody with him, of course."

"Well, that was pretty well established then,"

Trent remarked. "He was about as alone as he could be, it seems. Yet something happened somehow."

Mrs Hunt sniffed sceptically and lighted a cigarette. "Yes, it did," she said. "However, I didn't worry much about it, for one. Edith—Mrs Freer, that is, Royden's sister—must have had a terrible life of it with a man like that. Not that she ever said anything—she wouldn't. She is not that sort."

"She is a jolly good sort, anyhow," Hunt declared.

"Yes, she is; too good for most men. I can tell you," Mrs Hunt added for the benefit of Trent, "if Colin ever took to knocking me about, my well-known loyalty wouldn't stand the strain for very long."

"That's why I don't do it. It's the fear of exposure that makes me the perfect husband, Phil. She would tie a can to me before I knew what was happening. As for Edith, it's true she never said anything, but the change in her since it happened tells the story well enough. Since she's been living with her brother she has been looking far better and happier than she ever succeeded in doing while Freer was alive."

"She won't be living with him for very long, I dare say," Mrs Hunt intimated darkly.

"No. I'd marry her myself if I had the chance," Hunt agreed cordially.

"Pooh! You wouldn't be in the first six," his wife said. "It will be Rennie, or Gossett, or possibly Sandy Butler—you'll see. But perhaps you've had enough of the local tittle-tattle, Phil. Did you fix up a game for this afternoon?"

"Yes; with the Jarman Professor of Chemistry in the University of Cambridge," Trent said. "He looked at me as if he thought a bath of vitriol would do me good, but he agreed to play me."

"You've got a tough job," Hunt observed. "I believe he is almost as old as he looks, but he is a devil at the short game, and he knows the course blindfold, which you don't. And he isn't so cantankerous as he pretends to be. By the way, he was the man who saw the finish of the last shot Freer ever played—a sweet shot if ever there was one. Get him to tell you."

"I shall try to," Trent said. "The steward told me about that, and that was why I asked the professor for a game."

Colin Hunt's prediction was fulfilled that afternoon. Professor Hyde, receiving five strokes, was one up at the seventeenth, and at the last hole sent down a four-foot putt to win the match. As they left the green he remarked, as if in answer to something Trent had that moment said, "Yes; I can tell you a curious circumstance about Freer's death."

Trent's eye brightened; for the professor had not said a dozen words during their game, and Trent's tentative allusion to the subject after the second hole had been met merely by an intimidating grunt.

"I saw the finish of the last shot he played," the old gentleman went on, "without seeing the man himself at all. A lovely brassie it was, too—though lucky. Rolled to within two feet of the pin."

Trent considered. "I see," he said, "what you mean. You were near the second green, and the ball came over the ridge and ran down to the hole."

"Just so," Professor Hyde said. "That's how you play it—if you can. You might have done it yourself to-day, if your second shot had been thirty yards longer. I've never done it; but Freer often did. After a really good drive, you play a long second, blind, over the ridge; and with a perfect shot, you may get the green. Well, my house is quite near that green. I was pottering about in the garden before breakfast, and just as I happened to be looking towards the green a ball came hopping down the slope and trickled right across to the hole. Of course, I knew whose it must be—Freer always came along about that time. If it had been anyone else, I'd have waited to see him get his three, and congratulate him. As it was, I went indoors, and didn't hear of his death until long afterwards."

"And you never saw him play the shot?" Trent said thoughtfully.

The professor turned a choleric blue eye on him. "How the deuce could I?" he said huffily. "I can't see through a mass of solid earth."

"I know, I know," Trent said. "I was only trying to follow your mental process. Without seeing him play the shot, you knew it was his second—you say he would have been putting for a three. And you said, too—didn't you?—that it was a brassie shot."

"Simply because, my young friend"—the professor was severe—"I happened to know the man's game. I had played that nine holes with him before breakfast often, until one day he lost his temper more than usual, and made himself impossible. I knew he practically always carried the ridge with his second—I won't say he always got the green—and his brassie was the only club that would do it. It is conceivable, I admit," Professor Hyde added a little stiffly, "that some mishap took place and that the shot in question was not actually Freer's second; but it did not occur to me to allow for that highly speculative contingency."

On the next day, after those playing a morning round were started on their perambulation, Trent indulged himself with an hour's practice, mainly on the unsurveyed stretch of the second hole. Afterwards he had a word with the caddymaster; then visited the professional's shop, and won the regard of that expert by furnishing himself with a new mid-iron. Soon he brought up the subject of the last shot played by Arthur Freer. A dozen times that morning, he said, he had tried, after a satisfying drive, to reach the green with his second; but in vain. Fergus MacAdams shook his head. Not many, he said, could strike the ball with yon force. He could get there himself, whiles, but never for a certainty. Mr Freer had the strength, and he kenned how to use it forby.

What sort of clubs, Trent asked, had Freer preferred?

"Lang and heavy, like himsel'. . Noo ye mention it," MacAdam said, "I hae them here. They were brocht here after the ahccident." He reached up to the top of a rack. "Ay, here they are. They shouldna be, of course; but naebody came to claim them, and it juist slippit ma mind."

Trent, extracting the brassie, looked thoughtfully at the heavy head with the strip of hard white material inlaid in the face. "It's a powerful weapon, sure enough," he remarked.

"Ay, for a man that could control it," MacAdam said. "I dinna care for yon ivorine face mysel'. Some fowk think it gies mair reseelience, ye ken; but there's naething in it."

"He didn't get it from you, then," Trent suggested, still closely examining the head.

"Ay, but he did. I had a lot down from Nelsons while the fashion for them was on. Ye'll find my name," MacAdam added, "stampit on the wood in the usual place, if yer een are seein' richt."

"Well, I don't—that's just it. The stamp is quite illegible."

"Tod! Let's see," the professional said, taking the club in hand. "Guid reason for its being illegible," he went on after a brief scrutiny. "It's been obleeterated—that's easy seen. Who ever saw sic a daft-like thing! The wood has juist been crushed some gait—in a vice, I wouldna wonder. Noo, why would onybody want to dae a thing like yon?"

"Unaccountable, isn't it?" Trent said. "Still, it doesn't matter, I suppose. And anyhow, we shall never know."

It was twelve days later that Trent, looking in at the open door of the secretary's office, saw Captain Royden happily engaged with the separated parts of some mechanism in which coils of wire appeared to be the leading motive.

"I see you're busy," Trent said.

"Come in! Come in!" Royden said heartily. "I can do this any time—another hour's work will finish it." He laid down a pair of sharp-nosed pliers. "The electricity people have just changed us over to A.C., and I've got to re-wind the motor of our vacuum cleaner. Beastly nuisance," he added, looking down affectionately at the bewildering jumble of disarticulated apparatus on his table.

"You bear your sorrow like a man," Trent remarked; and Royden laughed as he wiped his hands on a towel.

"Yes," he said, "I do love tinkering about with mechanical jobs, and if I do say it myself, I'd rather do a thing like this with my own hands than risk having it faultily done by a careless workman. Too many of them about. Why, about a year ago the company sent a man here to fit a new main fuse-box, and he made a short-circuit with his screw-driver that knocked him right across the kitchen and might very well have killed him." He reached down his cigarette-box and offered it to Trent, who helped himself; then looked down thoughtfully at the device on the lid.

"Thanks very much. When I saw this box before, I put you down for an R.E. man. *Ubique*, and *Quo fas et gloria ducunt.* H'm! I wonder why Engineers were given that motto in particular.

"Lord knows," the captain said. "In my experience, sappers don't exactly go where right and glory lead. The dirtiest of all the jobs and precious little of the glory—that's what they get."

"Still, they have the consolation," Trent pointed

out, "of feeling that they are at home in a scientific age, and that all the rest of the army are amateurs compared with them. That's what one of them once told me, anyhow. Well now, captain, I have to be off this evening. I've looked in just to say how much I've enjoyed myself here."

"Very glad you did," Captain Royden said. "You'll come again, I hope, now you know that the golf here is not so bad."

"I like it immensely. Also the members. And the secretary." Trent paused to light his cigarette. "I found the mystery rather interesting, too."

Captain Royden's eyebrows lifted slightly. "You mean about Freer's death? So you made up your mind it *was* a mystery."

"Why, yes," Trent said. "Because I made up my mind he had been killed by somebody, and probably killed intentionally. Then, when I had looked into the thing a little, I washed out the 'probably'."

Captain Royden took up a penknife from his desk and began mechanically to sharpen a pencil. "So you don't agree with the coroner's jury?"

"No: as the verdict seems to have been meant to rule out murder or any sort of human agency, I don't. The lightning idea, which apparently satisfied them, or some of them, was not a very bright one, I thought. I was told what Dr Collins had said against it at the inquest; and it seemed to me he had disposed of it completely when he said that Freer's clubs, most of them steel ones, were quite undamaged. A man carrying his clubs puts them down, when he plays a shot, a few feet away at most; yet Freer was supposed to have been electrocuted without any notice having been taken of them, so to speak."

"H'm! No, it doesn't seem likely. I don't know that that quite decides the point, though," the captain said. "Lightning plays funny tricks, you know. I've seen a small tree struck when it was surrounded by trees twice the size. All the same, I quite agree there didn't seem to be any sense in the lightning notion. It was thundery weather, but there wasn't any storm that morning in this neighbourhood."

"Just so. But when I considered what had been said about Freer's clubs, it suddenly occurred to me that nobody had said anything about *the* club, so far as my information about the inquest went. It seemed clear, from what you and the parson saw, that he had just played a shot with his brassie when he was struck down; it was lying near him, not in the bag. Besides, old Hyde actually saw the ball he had hit roll down the slope on to the green. Now, it's a good rule to study every little detail when you are on a problem of this kind. There weren't many left to study, of course, since the thing had happened four months before; but I knew Freer's clubs must be somewhere, and I thought of one or two places where they were likely to have been taken, in the circumstances, so I tried them. First, I reconnoitred the caddy-master's shed, asking if I could leave my bag there for a day or two; but I was told that the regular place to leave them was the pro.'s shop. So I went and had a chat with MacAdam, and sure enough it soon came out that Freer's bag was still in his rack. I had a look at the clubs, too."

"And did you notice anything peculiar about them?" Captain Royden asked.

"Just one little thing. But it was enough to set me thinking, and next day I drove up to London, where I paid a visit to Nelsons, the sporting outfitters. You know the firm, of course."

Captain Royden, carefully fining down the point of his pencil, nodded. "Everybody knows Nelsons."

"Yes; and MacAdam, I knew, had an account there for his stocks. I wanted to look over some clubs of a particular make—a brassie, with a slip of ivorine let into the face, such as they had supplied to MacAdam. Freer had had one of them from him."

Again Royden nodded.

"I saw the man who shows clubs at Nelsons. We had a talk, and then—you know how little things come out in the course of conversation—"

"Especially," put in the captain with a cheerful grin, "when the conversation is being steered by an expert."

"You flatter me," Trent said. "Anyhow, it did transpire that a club of that particular make had been bought some months before by a customer whom the man was able to remember. Why he remembered him was because, in the first place, he insisted on a club of rather unusual length and weight—much too long and heavy for himself to use, as he was neither a tall man nor a powerful build. The salesman had suggested as much in a delicate way; but the customer said no, he knew exactly what suited him, and he bought the club and took it away with him."

"Rather an ass, I should say," Royden observed thoughtfully.

"I don't think he was an ass, really. He was capable of making a mistake, though, like the rest of us. There were some other things, by the way, that the salesman recalled about him. He had a slight limp, and he was, or had been, an army officer. The salesman was an ex-Service man, and he couldn't be mistaken, he said, about that."

Captain Royden had drawn a sheet of paper towards him, and was slowly drawing little geometrical figures as he listened. "Go on, Mr Trent," he said quietly.

"Well, to come back to the subject of Freer's death. I think he was killed by someone who knew Freer never played on Sunday, so that his clubs would be—or ought to be, shall we say?—in his locker all that day. All the following night, too, of course—in case the job took a long time. And I think this man was in a position to have access to the lockers in this clubhouse at any time he chose, and to possess a master-key to those lockers. I think he was a skilful amateur craftsman. I think he had a good practical knowledge of high explosives. There is a branch of the army"—Trent paused a moment and looked at the cigarette-box on the table—"in which that sort of knowledge is specially necessary, I believe."

Hastily, as if just reminded of the duty of hospitality, Royden lifted the lid of the box and pushed it towards Trent. "Do have another," he urged.

Trent did so with thanks. "They have to have it in the Royal Engineers," he went on, "because—so I'm told—demolition work is an important part of their job."

"Quite right," Captain Royden observed, delicately shading one side of a cube.

"*Ubique!*" Trent mused, staring at the box-lid. "If you are 'everywhere', I take it you can be in two places at the same time. You could kill a man in one place, and at the same time be having breakfast with a friend a mile away. Well, to return to our subject yet once more; you can see the kind of idea I was led to form about what happened to Freer. I believe that his brassie was taken from his locker on the Sunday before his death. I believe the ivorine face of it was taken off and a cavity hollowed out behind it; and in that cavity a charge of explosive was placed. Where it came from I don't know, for it isn't the sort of thing that is easy to come by, I imagine."

"Oh, there would be no difficulty about that," the captain remarked. "If this man you're speaking of knew all about H.E., as you say, he could have compounded the stuff himself from materials anybody can buy. For instance, he could easily make tetranitroaniline—that would be just the thing for him, I should say."

"I see. Then perhaps there would be a tiny detonator attached to the inner side of the ivorine face, so that a good smack with the brassie would set it off. Then the face would be fixed on again. It would be a delicate job, because the weight of the club-head would have to be exactly right. The feel and balance of the club would have to be just the same as before the operation."

"A delicate job, yes," the captain agreed. "But not an impossible one. There would be rather more to it than you say, as a matter of fact; the face would have to be shaved down thin, for instance. Still, it could be done."

"Well, I imagined it done. Now this man I have in mind knew there was no work for a brassie at the short first hole, and that the first time it would come out of the bag was at the second hole, down at the bottom of the dip, where no one could see what happened. What certainly did happen was that Freer played a sweet shot, slap on to the green. What else happened at the same moment we don't know for certain, but we can make a reasonable guess. And then, of course, there's the question of what happened to the club—or what was left of it; the handle, say. But it isn't a difficult question, I think, if we remember how the body was found."

"How do you mean?" Royden asked.

"I mean, by whom it was found. One of the two players who found it was too much upset to notice very much. He hurried back to the clubhouse; and the other was left alone with the body for, as I estimate it, at least fifteen minutes. When the police came on the scene, they found lying near the body a perfectly good brassie, an unusually long and heavy club, exactly like Freer's brassie in every respect—except one. The name stamped on the wood of the club-head had been obliterated by crushing. That name, I think, was not F. MacAdam, but W. J. Nelson; and the club had been taken out of a bag that was not Freer's—a bag which had the remains, if any, of Freer's brassie at the bottom of it. And I believe that's all." Trent got to his feet and stretched his arms. "You can see what I meant when I said I found the mystery interesting."

For some moments Captain Royden gazed thoughtfully out of the window; then he met Trent's inquiring eye. "If there was such a fellow as you imagine," he said coolly, "he seems to have been careful enough —lucky enough too, if you like—to leave nothing at all of what you could call proof against him. And probably he had personal and private reasons for what he did. Suppose that somebody whom he was much attached to was in the power of a foul-tempered, bullying brute; and suppose he found that the bullying had gone to the length of physical violence; and suppose that the situation was hell by day and by night to this man of yours; and suppose there was no way on earth of putting an end to it except the way he took. Yes, Mr Trent; suppose all that!"

"I will—I do!" Trent said. "That man—if he exists at all—must have been driven pretty hard, and what he did is no business of mine anyway. And now—still in the conditional mood—suppose I take myself off."

E. C. BENTLEY—*Trent Intervenes.*

THE VOYAGE

THE Picton boat was due to leave at half-past eleven. It was a beautiful night, mild, starry, only when they got out of the cab and started to walk down the Old Wharf that jutted out into the harbour, a faint wind blowing off the water ruffled under Fenella's hat, and she put up her hand to keep it on. It was dark on the Old Wharf, very dark; the wool sheds, the cattle trucks, the cranes standing up so high, the little squat railway engine, all seemed carved out of solid darkness. Here and there on a rounded wood-pile, that was like the stalk of a huge black mushroom, there hung a lantern, but it seemed afraid to unfurl its timid, quivering light in all that blackness; it burned softly, as if for itself.

Fenella's father pushed on with quick, nervous strides. Beside him her grandma bustled along in her crackling black ulster; they went so fast that she had now and again to give an undignified little skip to keep up with them. As well as her luggage strapped into a neat sausage, Fenella carried clasped to her her grandma's umbrella, and the handle, which was a swan's head, kept giving her shoulder a sharp little peck as if it too wanted her to hurry.
. . . Men, their caps pulled down, their collars turned up, swung by; a few women all muffled scurried along; and one tiny boy, only his little black arms and legs showing out of a white woolly

72

shawl, was jerked along angrily between his father and mother; he looked like a baby fly that had fallen into the cream.

Then suddenly, so suddenly that Fenella and her grandma both leapt, there sounded from behind the largest wool shed, that had a trail of smoke hanging over it, *Mia-oo-oo-O-O!*

"First whistle," said her father briefly, and at that moment they came in sight of the Picton boat. Lying beside the dark wharf, all strung, all beaded with round golden lights, the Picton boat looked as if she was more ready to sail among stars than out into the cold sea. People pressed along the gangway. First went her grandma, then her father, then Fenella. There was a high step down on to the deck, and an old sailor in a jersey standing by gave her his dry, hard hand. They were there; they stepped out of the way of the hurrying people, and standing under a little iron stairway that led to the upper deck they began to say good-bye.

"There, mother, there's your luggage!" said Fenella's father, giving grandma another strapped-up sausage.

"Thank you, Frank."

"And you've got your cabin tickets safe?"

"Yes, dear."

"And your other tickets?"

Grandma felt for them inside her glove and showed him the tips.

"That's right."

He sounded stern, but Fenella, eagerly watching him, saw that he looked tired and sad. *Mia-oo-oo-O-O!* The second whistle blared just above their heads, and a voice like a cry shouted, "Any more for the gangway?"

"You'll give my love to father," Fenella saw her father's lips say. And her grandma, very agitated, answered, "Of course I will, dear. Go now. You'll be left. Go now, Frank. Go now."

"It's all right, mother. I've got another three minutes." To her surprise Fenella saw her father take off his hat. He clasped grandma in his arms and pressed her to him. "God bless you, mother!" she heard him say.

And grandma put her hand, with the black thread glove that was worn through on her ring finger, against his cheek, and she sobbed, "God bless you, my own brave son!"

This was so awful that Fenella quickly turned her back on them, swallowed once, twice, and frowned terribly at a little green star on a mast head. But she had to turn round again; her father was going.

"Good-bye, Fenella. Be a good girl." His cold, wet moustache brushed her cheek. But Fenella caught hold of the lapels of his coat.

"How long am I going to stay?" she whispered anxiously. He wouldn't look at her. He shook her off gently, and gently said, "We'll see about that. Here! Where's your hand?" He pressed something into her palm. "Here's a shilling in case you should need it."

A shilling! She must be going away for ever! "Father!" cried Fenella. But he was gone. He was the last off the ship. The sailors put their shoulders to the gangway. A huge coil of dark rope went flying through the air and fell "thump" on the wharf. A bell rang; a whistle shrilled. Silently the dark wharf began to slip, to slide, to edge away from them. Now there was a rush of water between. Fenella strained to see with all her might. "Was that father turning round?"—or waving?—or standing alone?—or walking off by himself? The strip of water grew broader, darker. Now the Picton boat began to swing round steady, pointing out to sea. It was no good looking any longer. There was nothing to be seen but a few lights, the face of the town clock hanging in the air, and more lights, little patches of them, on the dark hills.

The freshening wind tugged at Fenella's skirts; she went back to her grandma. To her relief grandma seemed no longer sad. She had put the two sausages of luggage one on top of the other, and she was sitting on them, her hands folded, her head a little on one side. There was an intent, bright look on her face. Then Fenella saw that her lips were moving and guessed that she was praying. But the old woman gave her a bright nod as if to say the prayer was nearly over. She unclasped her hands, sighed, clasped them again, bent forward, and at last gave herself a soft shake.

"And now, child," she said, fingering the bow of her bonnet-strings, "I think we ought to see about our cabins. Keep close to me, and mind you don't slip."

"Yes, grandma!"

"And be careful the umbrellas aren't caught in the stair rail. I saw a beautiful umbrella broken in half like that on my way over."

"Yes, grandma."

75

Dark figures of men lounged against the rails. In the glow of their pipes a nose shone out, or the peak of a cap, or a pair of surprised-looking eyebrows. Fenella glanced up. High in the air, a little figure, his hands thrust in his short jacket pockets, stood staring out to sea. The ship rocked ever so little, and she thought the stars rocked too. And now a pale steward in a linen coat, holding a tray high in the palm of his hand, stepped out of a lighted doorway and skimmed past them. They went through that doorway. Carefully over the high brass-bound step on to the rubber mat and then down such a terribly steep flight of stairs that grandma had to put both feet on each step, and Fenella clutched the clammy brass rail and forgot all about the swan-necked umbrella.

At the bottom grandma stopped; Fenella was rather afraid she was going to pray again. But no, it was only to get out the cabin tickets. They were in the saloon. It was glaring bright and stifling; the air smelled of paint and burnt chop-bones and india-rubber. Fenella wished her grandma would go on, but the old woman was not to be hurried. An immense basket of ham sandwiches caught her eye. She went up to them and touched the top one delicately with her finger.

"How much are the sandwiches?" she asked.

"Tuppence!" bawled a rude steward, slamming down a knife and fork.

Grandma could hardly believe it.

"Twopence *each*?" she asked.

"That's right," said the steward, and he winked at his companion.

Grandma made a small, astonished face. Then she whispered primly to Fenella. "What wickedness!" And they sailed out at the further door and along a passage that had cabins on either side. Such a very nice stewardess came to meet them. She was dressed all in blue, and her collar and cuffs were fastened with large brass buttons. She seemed to know grandma well.

"Well, Mrs Crane," said she, unlocking their washstand. "We've got you back again. It's not often you give yourself a cabin."

"No," said grandma. "But this time my dear son's thoughtfulness——"

"I hope——" began the stewardess. Then she turned round and took a long mournful look at grandma's blackness and at Fenella's black coat and skirt, black blouse, and hat with a crape rose.

Grandma nodded. "It was God's will," said she.

The stewardess shut her lips and, taking a deep breath, she seemed to expand.

"What I always say is," she said, as though it was her own discovery, "sooner or later each of us has to go, and that's a certingty." She paused. "Now, can I bring you anything, Mrs Crane? A cup of tea? I know it's no good offering you a little something to keep the cold out."

Grandma shook her head. "Nothing, thank you. We've got a few wine biscuits, and Fenella has a very nice banana."

"Then I'll give you a look later on," said the stewardess, and she went out, shutting the door.

What a very small cabin it was! It was like being shut up in a box with grandma. The dark round

eye above the washstand gleamed at them dully.
Fenella felt shy. She stood against the door, still
clasping her luggage and the umbrella. Were they
going to get undressed in here? Already her grandma had taken off her bonnet, and, rolling up the
strings, she fixed each with a pin to the lining before
she hung the bonnet up. Her white hair shone like
silk; the little bun at the back was covered with a
black net. Fenella hardly ever saw her grandma
with her head uncovered; she looked strange.

"I shall put on the woollen fascinator your dear
mother crocheted for me," said grandma, and, un-
strapping the sausage, she took it out and wound it
round her head; the fringe of grey bobbles danced
at her eyebrows as she smiled tenderly and mourn-
fully at Fenella. Then she undid her bodice, and
something under that, and something else underneath that. Then there seemed a short, sharp
tussle, and grandma flushed faintly. Snip! Snap!
She had undone her stays. She breathed a sigh of
relief, and sitting on the plush couch, she slowly and
carefully pulled off her elastic-sided boots and stood
them side by side.

By the time Fenella had taken off her coat and
skirt and put on her flannel dressing-gown grandma
was quite ready.

"Must I take off my boots, grandma? They're
lace."

Grandma gave them a moment's deep consideration. "You'd feel a great deal more comfortable if
you did, child," said she. She kissed Fenella.
"Don't forget to say your prayers. Our dear Lord
is with us when we are at sea even more than when

we are on dry land. And because I am an experienced traveller," said grandma briskly, "I shall take the upper berth."

"But, grandma, however will you get up there?"

Three little spider-like steps were all Fenella saw. The old woman gave a small silent laugh before she mounted them nimbly, and she peered over the high bunk at the astonished Fenella.

"You didn't think your grandma could do that, did you?" said she. And as she sank back Fenella heard her light laugh again.

The hard square of brown soap would not lather, and the water in the bottle was like a kind of blue jelly. How hard it was, too, to turn down those stiff sheets; you simply had to tear your way in. If everything had been different, Fenella might have got the giggles. . . . At last she was inside, and while she lay there panting, there sounded from above a long, soft whispering, as though some one was gently, gently rustling among tissue paper to find something. It was grandma saying her prayers. . . .

A long time passed. Then the stewardess came in; she trod softly and leaned her hand on grandma's bunk.

"We're just entering the Straits," she said.

"Oh!"

"It's a fine night, but we're rather empty. We may pitch a little."

And indeed at that moment the Picton boat rose and rose and hung in the air just long enough to give a shiver before she swung down again, and there was the sound of heavy water slapping against her sides. Fenella remembered she had left that swan-necked umbrella standing up on the little couch. If it fell over, would it break? But grandma remembered too, at the same time.

"I wonder if you'd mind, stewardess, laying down my umbrella," she whispered.

"Not at all, Mrs Crane." And the stewardess, coming back to grandma breathed, "Your little granddaughter's in such a beautiful sleep."

"God be praised for that!" said grandma.

"Poor little motherless mite!" said the stewardess. And grandma was still telling the stewardess all about what happened when Fenella fell asleep.

But she hadn't been asleep long enough to dream before she woke up again to see something waving in the air above her head. What was it? What could it be? It was a small grey foot. Now another joined it. They seemed to be feeling about for something; there came a sigh.

"I'm awake, grandma," said Fenella.

"Oh, dear, am I near the ladder?" asked grandma. "I thought it was this end."

"No, grandma, it's the other. I'll put your foot on it. Are we there?" asked Fenella.

"In the harbour," said grandma. "We must get up, child. You'd better have a biscuit to steady yourself before you move."

But Fenella had hopped out of her bunk. The lamp was still burning, but night was over, and it was cold. Peering through that round eye, she could see far off some rocks. Now they were scattered over with foam; now a gull flipped by; and now there came a long piece of real land.

"It's land, grandma," said Fenella, wonderingly,

as though they had been at sea for weeks together. She hugged herself; she stood on one leg and rubbed it with the toes of the other foot; she was trembling. Oh, it had all been so sad lately. Was it going to change? But all her grandma said was, "Make haste, child. I should leave your nice banana for the stewardess as you haven't eaten it." And Fenella put on her black clothes again, and a button sprang off one of her gloves and rolled to where she couldn't reach it. They went up on deck.

But if it had been cold in the cabin, on deck it was like ice. The sun was not up yet, but the stars were dim, and the cold pale sky was the same colour as the cold pale sea. On the land a white mist rose and fell. Now they could see quite plainly dark bush. Even the shapes of the umbrella ferns showed, and those strange silvery withered trees that are like skeletons. . . . Now they could see the landing-stage and some little houses, pale too, clustered together, like shells on the lid of a box. The other passengers tramped up and down, but more slowly than they had the night before, and they looked gloomy.

And now the landing-stage came out to meet them. Slowly it swam towards the Picton boat, and a man holding a coil of rope, and a cart with a small drooping horse and another man sitting on the step, came too.

"It's Mr Penreddy, Fenella, come for us," said grandma. She sounded pleased. Her white waxen cheeks were blue with cold, her chin trembled, and she had to keep wiping her eyes and her little pink nose.

"You've got my—"

"Yes, grandma." Fenella showed it to her.

The rope came flying through the air, and "smack" it fell on to the deck. The gangway was lowered. Again Fenella followed her grandma on to the wharf over to the little cart, and a moment later they were bowling away. The hooves of the little horse drummed over the wooden piles, then sank softly into the sandy road. Not a soul was to be seen; there was not even a feather of smoke. The mist rose and fell, and the sea still sounded asleep as slowly it turned on the beach.

"I seen Mr Crane yestiddy," said Mr Penreddy. "He looked himself then. Missus knocked him up a batch of scones last week."

And now the little horse pulled up before one of the shell-like houses. They got down. Fenella put her hand on the gate, and the big, trembling dewdrops soaked through her glove-tips. Up a little path of round white pebbles they went, with drenched sleeping flowers on either side. Grandma's delicate white picotees were so heavy with dew that they were fallen, but their sweet smell was part of the cold morning. The blinds were down in the little house; they mounted the steps on to the verandah. A pair of old bluchers was on one side of the door, and a large red watering-can on the other.

"Tut! tut! Your grandpa," said grandma. She turned the handle. Not a sound. She called, "Walter!" And immediately a deep voice that sounded half stifled called back, "Is that you, Mary?"

"Wait, dear," said grandma. "Go in there."

She pushed Fenella gently into a small dusky sitting-room.

On the table a white cat, that had been folded up like a camel, rose, stretched itself, yawned, and then sprang on to the tips of its toes. Fenella buried one cold little hand in the white, warm fur, and smiled timidly while she stroked and listened to grandma's gentle voice and the rolling tones of grandpa.

A door creaked. "Come in, dear." The old woman beckoned, Fenella followed. There, lying to one side of an immense bed, lay grandpa. Just his head with a white tuft, and his rosy face and long silver beard showed over the quilt. He was like a very old wide-awake bird.

"Well, my girl!" said grandpa. "Give us a kiss!" Fenella kissed him. "Ugh!" said grandpa. "Her little nose is as cold as a button. What's that she's holding? Her grandma's umbrella?"

Fenella smiled again, and crooked the swan neck over the bed-rail. Above the bed there was a big text in a deep-black frame:

> *Lost! One Golden Hour*
> *Set with Sixty Diamond Minutes.*
> No *Reward Is Offered*
> *For It Is* GONE FOR EVER!

"Yer grandma painted that," said grandpa. And he ruffled his white tuft and looked at Fenella so merrily she almost thought he winked at her.

KATHERINE MANSFIELD—*The Garden Party.*

THE BLUE BEAD

From deep water came the crocodile.

Out of black water, carved with whirlpools, and into the frill of gold shallows by the stepping stones.

He was twice the length of a tall man; and inside him, among the stones which he had swallowed to aid digestion, rolled a silver bracelet.

Timber was being floated down this great Indian river from forests further up, and there were sleepers lying stuck round the stones until someone came to dislodge them and send them on their way, or until floods lifted them and jostled them along. The crocodile had no need to hide himself. He came to rest in the glassy shallows, among logs, and balanced there on tiptoe on the rippled sand, with only his raised eyes out of water, and raised nostrils breathing the clean sunny air.

Around him broad sparkling water travelled between cliffs and grass and forested hills. A jungle track came out of scrub each side and down to the sun-whitened stepping stones on which a little flycatcher was flirting and trilling along.

The mugger crocodile, blackish brown above and yellowy white under, lay motionless, able to wait for ever till food came. This antediluvian saurian—this prehistoric juggernaut, ferocious and formidable, a vast force in the water, propelled by the unimaginable and irresistible power of the huge tail, lay lapped by ripples, a throb in his throat. His mouth, running almost the whole length of his head, was closed and fixed in that evil bony smile, and where the yellow underside came up to it, it was tinged with green.

From the day, perhaps a hundred years ago, when the sun had hatched him in a sandbank, and he had broken his shell, and got his head out and looked round, ready to snap at anything before he was even fully hatched—from that day, when he had at once made for the water, ready to fend for himself immediately, he had lived by his brainless craft and ferocity. Escaping the birds of prey and the great carnivorous fishes that eat baby crocodiles, he had prospered, catching all the food he needed, and storing it till putrid in holes in the bank. Tepid water to live in, and plenty of rotted food grew him to his great length.

Now nothing could pierce the inch-thick armoured hide. Not even rifle bullets, which would bounce off. Only the eyes and the soft under-arms offered a place. He lived well in the river, sunning himself sometimes with other crocodiles—muggers, as well as the long-snouted fish-eating gharials—on warm rocks and sandbanks where the sun dried the clay on them quite white, and where they could plop off into the water in a moment if alarmed.

The big crocodile fed mostly on fish, but also on deer and monkeys come to drink, perhaps a duck or two. But sometimes here at the ford on a pi-dog full of parasites or a skeleton cow. And sometimes he went down to the burning ghats and found the half-burned bodies of Indians cast into the stream.

Beside him in the shoals as he lay waiting, glimmered a blue gem.

It was not a gem, though: it was sand-worn glass that had been rolling about in the river for a long time. By chance, it was perforated right through—the neck of a bottle perhaps?—a blue bead.

.   .   .   .   .

In the shrill noisy village above the ford, out of a mud house the same colour as the ground came a little girl, a thin starveling child dressed in an earth-coloured rag. She had torn the rag in two to make skirt and sari.

Sibia was eating the last of her meal, chupatti wrapped round a smear of green chilli and rancid butter; and she divided this also, to make it seem more, and bit it, showing straight white teeth.

With her ebony hair and great eyes, and her skin of oiled brown cream, she was a happy immature child-woman about twelve years old. Bare foot, of course, and often goosey-cold on a winter morning, and born to toil.

In all her life, she had never owned anything but a rag. She had never owned even one anna—not a pice, not a pi, even, to buy, say, a handful of blown glass beads from that stall in the bazaar where they were piled like stars, or one of the thin glass bangles that the man kept on a stick, and you could choose which colour you'd have.

She knew what finery was, though. She had been with her parents and brothers all through the jungle to the little town at railhead where there was this bazaar. And she had walked through all the milling people, and the dogs and monkeys full of fleas, the idling gossiping bargaining humanity spitting betel juice, heard the bell of a sacred bull clonking as he lumped along through the dust and hubbub.

She had paused, amazed, before the sweetmeat stall, to gaze at the brilliant honey confections, a-buzz with dust and flies. They smelled wonderful, above the smells of drains and humanity and cheap cigarettes. At home she sometimes tasted wild honey, or crunched the syrup out of a stalk of sugar cane. But these sweets were green and magenta.

Then there was the cloth stall, stacked with great rolls of new cotton cloth, stamped at the edge with the maker's sign of a tiger's head; and smelling so wonderful of its dressing, straight from the mills, that Sibia could have stood by it all day.

But there were other wonders to see: satin sewn with real silver thread, tin trays from Birmingham, and a sari which had got chips of looking-glass embroidered into the border. She joined the crowd round a Kashmiri travelling merchant on his way to the bungalows. He was showing dawn-coloured silks that poured like cream, and he'd got a little locked chest with turquoise and opals in it. Best of all, a box which, when you pressed it, a bell tinkled and a yellow woollen chicken jumped out.

There was no end to the wonders of the world.

But Sibia, in all her life from birth to death, was marked for work. Since she could toddle, she had husked corn, and gathered sticks, and put dung to dry, and cooked and weeded, and carried, and fetched water, and cut grass for fodder.

She was going with her mother and some other women now to get paper grass from the cliffs above the river. When you had enough of it, you could take it down by bullock cart to railhead and sell it to the agent who would arrange for its dispatch to the paper mills. The women often toiled all day at this work, and the agent sat on silk cushions, smoking a hookah.

Such thoughts did not trouble Sibia, however, as she skipped along with her sickle and home-made hayfork beside her mother. You could skip on the way out, but not on the way back when you ached with tiredness, and there was a great load to carry.

Some of the women were wearing necklaces made out of lal-lal-beeges, the shiny scarlet seeds, black one end, that grew everywhere in the jungle—it was best to have new necklaces each year, instead of last year's faded ones—and Sibia was making one too. How nice it was going to be to hear that rattling swish round her neck, as she froushed along with lots of necklaces. But each seed, hard as stone, had to be drilled with a red-hot needle, and the family needle was snapped, so she must wait till they could buy another.

Oh for strings and strings of glass and beads — anklets, ear-rings, nose-rings, bangles — all the gorgeous dazzle of the bazaar—all her little golden body decorated!

Chattering as they went, the women followed the dusty track towards the river. On their way, they passed a Gujar encampment of grass huts where these nomadic graziers would live for a time until their animals had perhaps finished all the easy grazing within reach, or they were not able to sell enough of their white butter and white milk in the district, or there was no one to buy the young male buffaloes for tiger-bait. Or perhaps a cattle-killing tiger was making a nuisance of himself. Then they'd move on.

Sibia glanced at the Gujar women as she went past. They wore trousers, tight and wrinkled at the ankles, and in their ears large silver rings made out of melted rupees; and one of them was clinking a stick against the big brass gurrahs in which they fetched water from the river for the camp, to see which ones were empty. The men and boys were out of camp just now with the herd or gone to the bazaar to sell produce, but one or two buffaloes were standing about, creatures of great wet noses and moving jaws and gaunt black bones.

The Gujars were junglis, as Sibia was too, born and bred in the forest. For countless centuries, their forbears had lived like this, getting their living from animals, from grass and trees, as they scratched their food together, and stored their substance in large herds and silver jewelry. They were Man in the wandering Pastoral Age, not Stone Age hunters, and not yet Cultivators.

Ah, now there was the river, twinkling between the trees, sunlit beyond dark trunks. They could hear it rushing along.

The women came out on the shore, and made for the stepping stones.

They had plenty to laugh and bicker about, as they approached the river in a noisy crowd. They girded up their skirts, so as to jump from stone to

stone, and they clanked their sickles and forks
together over their shoulders to have ease of movement. They shouted their quarrels above the gush
of the river.

Noise frightens crocodiles. The big mugger did
not move, and all the women crossed in safety to the
other bank.

Here they had to climb stiff hillsides to get at the
grass, but all fell to with a will, and sliced away at it
wherever there was foothold to be had.

Down below them ran the broad river, pouring
powerfully out from its deep narrow pools among the
cold cliffs and shadows, spreading into warm
shallows, lit by kingfishers. Great turtles lived
there, and mahseer weighing more than a hundred
pounds. Crocodiles too. Sometimes you could see
them lying out on those slabs of clay over there, but
there were none to be seen at the moment.

Where Sibia was working, wind coming across
hundreds of miles of trees cooled her sweating body,
and she could look down over the river as if she were
a bird. Although she did not dare stop for a moment
under her mother's eye, her imagination took her
in swooping flight over the bright water and golden
air to the banks where she had played as a child.

In those cavelets above the high water mark of the
highest flood, she had stored some little bowls
moulded of clay while they hardened. If there
were anything that could be used for colouring,
they would look fine, painted with marigolds and
elephants.

"Child!"

The sharp word—the glare of her mother's angry

sweating face, pulled Sibia back to work, and they toiled on.

But at last it was time to go back to see to their animals and the evening meal. The loaded women set out to cross the river again.

Sibia hung back. She would just dawdle a bit and run and see if the little clay cups were still there in the cave, waiting to be painted and used.

Although the women were now tired and loaded, they still talked. Those in front yelled to those behind. They crossed the river safely and disappeared up the track into the trees on the other side. Even their voices died away.

Silence fell.

Sibia came down alone to the stepping stones.

The light of evening was striking up the gorge, pink into the ultra-violet shadows. Now that the sun was off it, the water poured almost invisible among the stones, with no reflection to show where it began.

Sibia stepped on to the first stone.

She was heavily weighted, her muscles stretched and aching. The hayfork squeaked in the packed dry grass and dug into her collar bone so close under the skin, in spite of the sari bunched up to make a pad.

When she was half way over, she put her load down on a big boulder to rest; and leant, breathing, on the fork.

At the same moment a Gujar woman came down with two gurrahs to the water on the other side. In order to get the good clear water, which would quickly fill both gurrahs to the top without sand, she walked on to the stepping stones.

She was within a yard of the crocodile when he lunged at her.

Up out of the darkling water heaved the great reptile, water slushing off him, his livid jaws yawning and all his teeth flashing as he slashed at her leg.

The woman screamed, dropped both brass pots with a clatter on the boulder, from whence they bounced to the water and Sibia saw them bob away in the current. *Oh the two good vessels gone.*

The Gujar woman recoiled from the crocodile, but his jaws closed on her leg at the same moment as she slipped and fell on the bone-breaking stone, and clutched one of the timber logs to save herself.

The log jammed between two boulders, with the woman clinging to it and screaming, while the crocodile pulled on her leg, threshing his mighty tail—bang!—bang!—to and fro in great smacking flails as he tried to drag her free and carry her off down into the deeps of the pool. Blood spread everywhere.

Sibia sprang.

From boulder to boulder she came leaping like a rock goat. Sometimes it had seemed difficult to cross these stones, especially the big gap in the middle where the river coursed through like a bulge of glass. But now she came on wings, choosing her footing in mid air without even thinking about it, and in one moment she was beside the shrieking woman.

In the boiling bloody water, the face of the crocodile, fastened round her leg, was tugging to and fro, and smiling.

His eyes rolled round on to Sibia. One slap of the tail could kill her.

He struck. Up shot the water, twenty feet, and fell like a silver chain.

Again!

The rock jumped under the blow.

But in the daily heroism of the jungle, as common as a thorn tree, Sibia did not hesitate.

She aimed at the reptile's eyes.

With all the force of her little body, she drove the hayfork at the eyes, and one prong went in—right in—while its pair scratched past on the horny cheek.

The crocodile reared up in convulsion, till half his lizard body was out of the river, the tail and nose nearly meeting over his stony back. Then he crashed back, exploding the water, and in an uproar of bloody foam he disappeared.

He would die. Not yet, but presently, though his death would not be known for days; not till his stomach, blown with gas, floated him. Then perhaps he would be found upside down among the logs at the timber boom, with pus in his eye.

Sibia got her arms round the fainting woman, and somehow dragged her from the water. She stopped her wounds with sand, and bound them with rag, and helped her home to the Gujar encampment where the men made a litter to carry her to someone for treatment.

Then Sibia went back for her grass and sickle and fork.

The fork was lying in the river, not carried away, luckily, and as she bent to pick it up out of the water, she saw the blue bead. Not blue now, with the sun nearly gone, but a no-colour white-blue, and its shape wobbling in the movement of the stream.

She reached her arm down into a yard of the cold silk water to get it. Missing it first of all, because of refraction.

Then there it lay in her wet palm, perfect, even pierced ready for use, with the sunset shuffled about inside it like gold-dust. All her heart went up in flames of joy.

After a bit she twisted it into the top of her skirt against her tummy so she would know if it burst through the poor cloth and fell.

Then she picked up her fork and sickle and the heavy grass and set off home. Ai! Ai! What a day!

Her bare feet smudged out the wriggle-mark of snakes in the dust; there was the thin singing of malaria mosquitoes among the trees now; and this track was much used at night by a morose old makna elephant—the Tuskless One; but Sibia was not thinking of any of them. The stars came out: she did not notice.

On the way back she met her mother, out of breath, come to look for her, and scolding.

"I did not see till I was home, that you were not there. I thought something must have happened to you."

And Sibia, bursting with her story, cried "Something *did!* I found a blue bead for my necklace, look!"

NORAH BURKE—*The Blue Bead.*

FEAR [1]

On the horizon three separate thunderstorms talked darkly to each other.

The hut where little Richard and his grandfather had taken shelter was already green with darkness, its air stifling and warm, and the trees that surrounded it purple and heavy with whispers. When the boy heard sounds coming from the wood he would turn upwards a pair of great eyes, faint-yellow with fear, and ask in an awed way:

"What's the matter, grandfather? What makes it dark?"

Sometimes the man would scratch his beard and say nothing, at another grunt and say, "Don't you worry yourself," and at a third, "You ain't frightened, are you? You're too big a boy to be frightened. You sit still. You'll wear your breeches out."

But the child would never cease to cast his great swollen eyes about the hut, fidget on trembling haunches, and show that he was afraid of the silent darkness and the growls of thunder which dropped into it, reminding him of the voices of cows and dogs. Thus he saw nothing tiresome in repeating:

"What's the matter, grandfather? What makes it dark?"

Each time he said this there seemed less to be seen in the hut, and not much outside, either, where the three thunder-storms grew angrier and angrier with each other. In the wood the trees began to open their arms in readiness to catch the approaching rain. When this did not come the old man wetted his soft lips, told the boy he would sing him something, and began a ballad.

Beyond the first note or two, however, the boy did not listen, and in a few moments the thin tune gave up its exploration of the stagnant air, and the man said again:

"You sit still. There's nothing to hurt."

"What's it dark for, then?" persisted the boy.

"It's going to rain," he was told.

He could not understand this.

"Yesterday it rained and the sun shone," he said. "Why doesn't the sun shine now?"

"The sun ain't here."

"Then where's it gone?" he naïvely asked.

"Don't you worry."

And again it thundered. Now the boy could scarcely see his grandfather. When all was silent again he went to the door and peeped out.

"What makes the sky green?" he asked.

"It ain't green!" his grandfather declared.

"It is," he persisted. "It's green like Nancy's hat. What makes it green?"

"It's going to rain," was the answer. "That's all. You be quiet."

He wept in reply. As he looked up through the film of his tears it seemed as if the black sky was pushing the trees down on the hut, and that before long they would crush it and bury him. "I want to go home," he whispered, but the man did not answer. For a long time there was a sultry silence. The boy felt himself sweating, and could not see his grandfather. Suddenly it began to rain, at first desultorily, then thickly and with a great hissing sound.

"Grandfather! Grandfather!" He wept and ran at last between the man's dark knees. "Grandfather!" he whimpered.

There were sleepy grunts in reply.

"Wake up!" the little one whispered. "It's raining. I want to go home. Wake up!"

When the old man aroused himself it was to hear immense shaking rolls of thunder, the boy's voice in tears, and the rain throwing itself against the window in a sort of grey passion.

"I want to go home!" the boy cried. "It's night. Mamma'll have gone to bed."

"You be quiet," comforted the man. "It ain't night."

"Then what time is it?"

Like a white eye a watch came out in the gloom. Then a bluish match-flame spurted over it, and for a minute the boy, gazing silently at the leaf-shaped light and its reflections on his grandfather's face and the roof of the hut, momentarily forgot the storm and his fear.

"It's only eight o'clock," his grandfather growled. "You sit quiet."

But at that moment the flame seemed to be swallowed by the darkness and, as if by some malicious miracle, next moment to appear again in a frenzied light that gave the sky a yellow wound which in turn spilt yellow blood on the wood and the dark floor of the hut. There came thunder, as if a great beast sat roaring on the roof. The hot peaceable air seemed to cry out like a sensitive child. The trees were distressed, the great confusion made the boy's head thick and hot with terror.

He buried his head in the friendly cavern between the man's thighs and there groaned and wept in darkness.

And as the thunder and lightning made their terrifying duet above his head, he tried to think of his home, his mother's cool face, and the windows where there were blinds and harmless moths. But he managed it all vaguely, and felt that what prevented him was the storm, which was something black and cunning and old, and from which he had not a chance of escape. Only if he remained half-eaten up by the shadows and were mistaken for a dog or sack might he perhaps escape. And so he crouched there, very still, trying not to listen, but hearing everything in a greater tumult than ever, and knew that the storm went on without heeding his fear.

Nearly an hour passed : often the boy wanted to cry out, but felt as if choked by fear and darkness and kept silent. His knees grew cold, and one leg fell into a tingling sleep. Only his head was warm and throbbed madly like an old clock. . . . Once there was a smell of burning from the wood, but it passed, and the boy forgot it in wondering if animals were terrified as he was, and where all the birds had gone, and why they were silent. . . . Then by some lucky chance he caught the silvery ticks of his grandfather's watch and was comforted.

So it grew quiet and a clear darkness came. The boy got up and opened his eyes. The rain no longer growled, and soon the thunder passed off. Outside the cobwebs hung like ropes of leaden beads, and the ground was covered with great shadow-printed pools over which the man lifted the boy. From the edge of the wood were visible the blue storms, retreated far off in a mist, and a star or two in the course they had used.

"There's the cuckoo!" the man said.

It was true, and as the boy listened he forgot the last of his fear. When he tried to walk he discovered his legs were stiff, and that when he set it down one foot tingled as if a thousand pins had been pressed into it, and he laughed.

For diversion the man told old stories, which the child heard vaguely, and, when that grew stale, held the boy's forefinger in his own rugged palm and counted the stars.

"Fifty-one . . . fifty-two."

And though once or twice lightning flashed afar off, there was no thunder. As the stars increased it seemed to the boy that the storm had lost all terror for him, that perhaps he had been asleep when the most terrible flashes came, and that soon the village would come, and from then onwards no fear.

"I'm not frightened, grandfather," he said, a dozen times.

Then, as it struck nine o'clock, and the boy listened to the notes roaming about the dark fields, he saw a star shoot.

"A star fell down! A star fell down!" he immediately cried. "Oh, golly!"

He was seized with joy, punched the man's legs, jumped into a pool, and cried again:

"A star fell down!"

But his grandfather said nothing.

He did not thoroughly believe in the superstition that a falling star means death, but for some reason he could not help thinking of the connection between the two. As he went down the hill his mind became restive. Suddenly he thought of his wife, of her death, then of his own age, then of his stale limbs and the possibility of his dying before another day. Gradually it seemed he was doomed to die soon. He began to sweat, just as the boy had done, and was obsessed by the idea of something terrible and black waiting in readiness to crush the life from him, and against which there was no chance for body and soul. . . .

One or two birds began to chirp. The boy heard them, but, like the man, thought only of the star. He remembered he must ask if animals were afraid, and where birds hid during the storm, but looking up into his grandfather's face saw it serious with shadows, and dared only say:

"Did you see the star fall?"

There was no reply. As they walked down the hill the man became more and more stricken by the fear of death, and could not hold himself still. But the boy would only laugh, and, while watching for other stars to shoot, wonder, with perplexity in his eyes, why his grandfather looked stern and miserable, and, hurrying along as if it were going to rain again, never spoke to him.

H. E. Bates—*The Best Short Stories of* 1927.

THE LUNCHEON

I CAUGHT sight of her at the play and in answer to her beckoning I went over during the interval and sat down beside her. It was long since I had last seen her and if someone had not mentioned her name I hardly think I would have recognised her. She addressed me brightly.

"Well, it's many years since we first met. How time does fly! We're none of us getting any younger. Do you remember the first time I saw you? You asked me to luncheon."

Did I remember?

It was twenty years ago and I was living in Paris. I had a tiny apartment in the Latin Quarter over-looking a cemetery and I was earning barely enough money to keep body and soul together. She had read a book of mine and had written to me about it. I answered, thanking her, and presently I received from her another letter saying that she was passing through Paris and would like to have a chat with me; but her time was limited and the only free moment she had was on the following Thursday; she was spending the morning at the Luxembourg and would I give her a little luncheon at Foyot's afterwards? Foyot's is a restaurant at which the French senators eat and it was so far beyond my means that I had never even thought of going there. But I was flattered and I was too young to have learned to say no to a woman. (Few men, I may add, learn this until they are too old to make it of any consequence to a woman what they say.) I had eighty francs (gold francs) to last me the rest of the month and a modest luncheon should not cost more than fifteen. If I cut out coffee for the next two weeks I could manage well enough.

I answered that I would meet my friend—by correspondence—at Foyot's on Thursday at half-past twelve. She was not so young as I expected and in appearance imposing rather than attractive. She was in fact a woman of forty (a charming age, but not one that excites a sudden and devastating passion at first sight), and she gave me the impression of having more teeth, white and large and even, than were necessary for any practical purpose. She was talkative, but since she seemed inclined to talk about me I was prepared to be an attentive listener.

I was startled when the bill of fare was brought, for the prices were a great deal higher than I had anticipated. But she reassured me.

"I never eat anything for luncheon," she said.

"Oh, don't say that!" I answered generously.

"I never eat more than one thing. I think people eat far too much nowadays. A little fish, perhaps. I wonder if they have any salmon."

Well, it was early in the year for salmon and it was not on the bill of fare, but I asked the waiter if there was any. Yes, a beautiful salmon had just come in, it was the first they had had. I ordered it for my guest. The waiter asked her if she would have something while it was being cooked.

"No," she answered, "I never eat more than one

thing. Unless you had a little caviare. I never mind caviare."

My heart sank a little. I knew I could not afford caviare, but I could not very well tell her that. I told the waiter by all means to bring caviare. For myself I chose the cheapest dish on the menu and that was a mutton chop.

"I think you're unwise to eat meat," she said. "I don't know how you can expect to work after eating heavy things like chops. I don't believe in overloading my stomach."

Then came the question of drink.

"I never drink anything for luncheon," she said.

"Neither do I," I answered promptly.

"Except white wine," she proceeded as though I had not spoken. "These French white wines are so light. They're wonderful for the digestion."

"What would you like?" I asked, hospitable still, but not exactly effusive.

She gave me a bright and amicable flash of her white teeth.

"My doctor won't let me drink anything but champagne."

I fancy I turned a trifle pale. I ordered half a bottle. I mentioned casually that my doctor had absolutely forbidden me to drink champagne.

"What are you going to drink, then?"

"Water."

She ate the caviare and she ate the salmon. She talked gaily of art and literature and music. But I wondered what the bill would come to. When my mutton chop arrived she took me quite seriously to task.

"I see that you're in the habit of eating a heavy luncheon. I'm sure it's a mistake. Why don't you follow my example and just eat one thing? I'm sure you'd feel ever so much better for it."

"I *am* only going to eat one thing," I said, as the waiter came again with the bill of fare.

She waved him aside with an airy gesture.

"No, no, I never eat anything for luncheon. Just a bite, I never want more than that, and I eat that more as an excuse for conversation than anything else. I couldn't possibly eat anything more—unless they had some of those giant asparagus. I should be sorry to leave Paris without having some of them."

My heart sank. I had seen them in the shops and I knew that they were horribly expensive. My mouth had often watered at the sight of them.

"Madame wants to know if you have any of those giant asparagus," I asked the waiter.

I tried with all my might to will him to say no. A happy smile spread over his broad, priest-like face, and he assured me that they had some so large, so splendid, so tender, that it was a marvel.

"I'm not in the least hungry," my guest sighed, "but if you insist I don't mind having some asparagus."

I ordered them.

"Aren't you going to have any?"

"No, I never eat asparagus."

"I know there are people who don't like them. The fact is, you ruin your palate by all the meat you eat."

We waited for the asparagus to be cooked. Panic seized me. It was not a question now how much money I should have left over for the rest of the month, but whether I had enough to pay the bill. It would be mortifying to find myself ten francs short and be obliged to borrow from my guest. I could not bring myself to do that. I knew exactly how much I had and if the bill came to more I made up my mind that I would put my hand in my pocket and with a dramatic cry start up and say it had been picked. Of course it would be awkward if she had not money enough either to pay the bill. Then the only thing would be to leave my watch and say I would come back and pay later.

The asparagus appeared. They were enormous, succulent and appetising. The smell of the melted butter tickled my nostrils as the nostrils of Jehovah were tickled by the burned offerings of the virtuous Semites. I watched the abandoned woman thrust them down her throat in large voluptuous mouthfuls and in my polite way I discoursed on the condition of the drama in the Balkans. At last she finished.

"Coffee?" I said.

"Yes, just an ice-cream and coffee," she answered.

I was past caring now, so I ordered coffee for myself and an ice-cream and coffee for her.

"You know, there's one thing I thoroughly believe in," she said, as she ate the ice-cream. "One should always get up from a meal feeling one could eat a little more."

"Are you still hungry?" I asked faintly.

"Oh, no, I'm not hungry; you see, I don't eat luncheon. I have a cup of coffee in the morning and then dinner, but I never eat more than one thing for luncheon. I was speaking for you."

"Oh, I see!"

Then a terrible thing happened. While we were waiting for the coffee, the head waiter, with an ingratiating smile on his false face, came up to us bearing a large basket full of huge peaches. They had the blush of an innocent girl; they had the rich tone of an Italian landscape. But surely peaches were not in season then? Lord knew what they cost. I knew too—a little later, for my guest, going on with her conversation, absentmindedly took one.

"You see, you've filled your stomach with a lot of meat"—my one miserable little chop—"and you can't eat any more. But I've just had a snack and I shall enjoy a peach."

The bill came and when I paid it I found that I had only enough for a quite inadequate tip. Her eyes rested for an instant on the three francs I left for the waiter and I knew that she thought me mean. But when I walked out of the restaurant I had the whole month before me and not a penny in my pocket.

"Follow my example," she said as we shook hands, "and never eat more than one thing for luncheon."

"I'll do better than that," I retorted. "I'll eat nothing for dinner to-night."

"Humorist!" she cried gaily, jumping into a cab. "You're quite a humorist!"

But I have had my revenge at last. I do not believe that I am a vindictive man, but when the immortal gods take a hand in the matter it is pardonable to observe the result with complacency. To-day she weighs twenty-one stone.

W. SOMERSET MAUGHAM—
The Complete Short Stories. Volume One.

THE MAN WHO STOLE THE PELICAN

Sir Charles Trumpington, permanent Chief of His Majesty's Diplomatic Office, was in a quandary. He knew very well that the foolscap envelope, which lay unopened on his desk, contained his emissary's secret report on the recent murders at Tresbon, the capital of Zenobia. He recognized the writing of the address, and, moreover, the report was expected. But, on the other hand, he had not expected this report—a document the secrecy of which was of international importance—to reach him for at least another two days. On Wednesday, at the earliest, he had thought that it might arrive; and now there it was staring him in the face, at ten o'clock on Monday morning. It was most annoying.

"Confound Travers!" thought Sir Charles, "I wish he were sometimes not quite so speedy in carrying out his instructions!"

For the fact was, much as Trumpington wished for this report, he was expecting a visit, in half an hour's time, from the Zenobian Ambassador: and he particularly wished to be able to assure His Excellency that no reliable account of the Tresbon murders had yet reached London. That would enable him to give the Ambassador a chance of explaining the affair, and would also allow Trumpington to estimate how honestly Zenobia intended to act by Great Britain in this troublesome affair.

It would, of course, be quite possible to read the report, and still assert to his visitor that he had not done so. But Trumpington had the peculiar cast of mind that dislikes the lie direct—even in a good cause—and he therefore sought for some less blatantly untruthful way out of his difficulty. He would put the document, still unopened and unread, in his safe. That would do, at a pinch, though he would not feel particularly comfortable about it. Supposing the Ambassador were to word his questions awkwardly, and ask, for instance: "Do you mean to assure me, Sir Charles, that you have no report on these regrettable incidents"—he would hardly use the word *murders*—"in your files?" To answer such a question would certainly entail some violence to Sir Charles Trumpington's conscience—a part of his being which he treated—perhaps in reaction against the general standards of diplomacy—with a tenderness which amounted almost to cosseting.

No, he reflected, that would hardly do. The lie direct he would avoid, if he possibly could. It would be better to get the wretched report clear out of the building; and then, unless the Ambassador were so unfortunate in his choice of phrases as to use the verb *receive*—"Have you not *received* an account?"—he might get out of the affair without a stain upon his character. The reader will perhaps think that a diplomatist's conscience was hardly worth so much thought, such long consideration; but this was not the view of Sir Charles Trumpington. He finally decided to have the inopportune document removed, temporarily, from the Diplomatic Office, and he therefore rang the bell.

"Ask Mr Tape to step this way," he said to the commissionaire who answered his ring.

Two minutes later Mr Michael Tape made his appearance. "Ah, Tape," said the chief, affably, but yet with a touch of nervousness in his manner, "nothing of any special importance in this morning, I suppose?"

"Nothing particular, sir."

"Well—er—well—the fact is, Tape, it would be a considerable convenience to me if you would condescend to take the morning off to-day."

Tape looked surprised. "Take the morning off, sir," he repeated incredulously.

"Yes, quite so," replied Sir Charles. "Go out for a walk. It's a nice sunny morning. Go anywhere you like. And, by the way, you might slip this letter in your pocket before you go—but mind you take the greatest possible care of it—the very greatest care. Guard it as you would your honour. Your life, I mean," he corrected, thinking, no doubt, that the latter was a more intrinsically valuable commodity.

Tape took the envelope. Travers's writing, he knew; and he also knew of the Tresbon murders, the Zenobian Ambassador's impending call, and the line his chief intended to take at the interview. He had, in addition, a fairly accurate appreciation of Sir Charles Trumpington's mental habits. So he was able to grasp the situation.

"I understand, sir," he said, slipping the precious envelope into the inside breast pocket of his jacket.

Sir Charles looked somewhat pained at his subordinate's remark.

"I don't know, Mr Tape," he said stiffly, "that there is any need for you to understand. That will do for the present. Go out immediately, and be back with Travers's rep—er, I mean, with the envelope, at two o'clock."

Michael Tape retired, fetched his hat and stick from his own room, and left the building. He strolled along Whitehall a short way, then turned through the Horse Guards Arch and sauntered idly into St James's Park. He was a man of about forty years of age, inclining to stoutness, and of somewhat fastidious tastes. His hair was well-brushed and black in colour—though the latter fact did not prevent certain of his more jocose friends from seizing the obvious opportunity afforded by his surname, and by his employment in the Civil Service, to the extent of calling him "Red Tape" in playful moments. This annoyed Michael, though he tried not to show it.

Perhaps because a career in the Diplomatic Office left him little faith in human nature, Michael Tape's passion in life was the study of birds and beasts of all sorts. Every Sunday afternoon, for example, he would wander round the Zoo, and he was known to all the keepers there as one of the more instructed of the regular visitors of the Gardens. Most of his meditations centred round animals of various sorts, and sometimes he would imagine himself going on romantic expeditions to distant parts of the world and returning with strange and rare beasts and birds for the collection in Regent's Park. It was one of his daydreams to see the magic phrase "Presented by Michael Tape, Esq., F.Z.S.," painted upon

innumerable little tin labels. This morning, however, he did not go to the Zoo, but into St James's
Park, to visit his old friends the pelicans.

He was, apparently, in luck, for half a dozen of
those admirably grotesque birds had left the water
of the lake and were sunning themselves on the grass
close to the railings, against which Tape leaned idly,
watching the pompous movements of the pelicans.
One of them had carried a small fish along from the
water, but had dropped it on the turf without
swallowing it, for pelicans, as anyone who has
watched them knows, are fond of toying with their
food—tossing it up in the air and catching it, then
dropping it again—before finally making a meal of
it. Tape thought it would be amusing to get hold
of the fish and to hold it up by the tail for one of the
birds to catch. He therefore bent over the rails
and tried to draw the fish near to him with his stick.
This manœuvre attracted the attention of the
pelicans, who came poking round his stick, making
clacking noises with their long bills.

Then, while this entertaining sport was at its
height, a horrible thing happened. The precious
envelope, with Travers's secret report inside it,
slipped out of Tape's pocket and fell right in front
of the assembled pelicans.

This, in itself, would not have been a terribly
serious matter, had not one of the birds taken into its
head the perverse idea that the wretched envelope
might make a pleasant change from a diet of fish.
With this in mind, and before Tape could rescue his
precious charge, the pelican in question had seized
the envelope, had tossed it up in the air, had caught

it adroitly, and was holding it in his bill. Tape was horrified.

"Give it here," he shouted to the bird. But shouting did no good, the bird merely once more threw the thing up and caught it.

Tape tried persuasion. "Pretty Pelly," he coaxed, working upon an obvious analogy, "there's a good Pelly. There's a nice bird." And he held out his hand, hoping, supposedly, that the pelican would hand the document back to him.

But no miracle of the kind happened; persuasion was as useless as shouting; and the pelican, deciding to taste this strange titbit, incontinently bolted the envelope. Into the pouch it went, then it could be seen travelling down the throat, and finally it disappeared into the innermost portions of the bird's anatomy.

This was a disaster indeed. Tape could see his whole career disappearing in the crop of the pelican, which, together with its companions, was now waddling towards the lake. What was to be done? No park-keeper was in sight to whom Tape could appeal for aid; and he knew that if he once took his eye off the identical bird that contained Travers's report (he had heard of documents being digested, but never before in quite this way) he would not recognize it from its fellows, and the whole flock might have to be slaughtered in order to recover the lost document. At this thought he quailed; to have his six beloved pelicans butchered was more than he could have stood, even had he thought that he could have persuaded the park authorities to do it. He must come to a decision, at once; and this necessity being forced upon him, he did so. He vaulted, with surprising agility, over the railings, rushed towards the pelican and, remembering his early achievements as a Rugby football player, threw himself full length after it, clasping it round the neck and shoulders.

But the pelican was not for surrendering without a struggle, and for a minute or so bird and civil servant rolled about this way and that on the grass, the former emitting loud squawks and the latter puffing and snorting like a thousand grampuses. But eventually Tape had the better of it, and managed to get on his feet, still clasping the struggling bird to his breast.

A pelican, it will readily be understood, is no mean weight, but Tape succeeded in clambering back across the railings without losing his prisoner. Luckily the park was almost deserted, but one male loafer and a couple of nursemaids had now appeared on the scene, and in the far, far distance our hero could see a policeman making as hurried an approach as dignity would permit. Tape realized, therefore, that in a few moments authority would arrive, and would certainly prevent his kidnapping project. But it was only a few yards to the road, along which he could see a disengaged taxi driving slowly in his direction. To the taxi, then, he bolted, the terrified bird fighting all the while to get free of his clutches, and making all the noises its capacious throat could command.

Michael Tape, however, was made of stern stuff, and kept a firm grasp of his lively burden. Gasping for breath he tottered to the taxi (which the driver had pulled up in astonishment) and pushed the bird, beak foremost, in through the fortunately open window.

The driver began to protest, but Tape cut him short with the magic phrase "Three times your fare!" and then tried to get into the car himself. But the pelican, apparently, was of another opinion, and every time the luckless Michael put his foot inside the door he found his leg painfully assaulted with all the violence of which that very powerful beak was capable. Yet the policeman (who had accelerated his pace) was now within thirty yards, things were almost desperate, and into the cab Michael plunged, to the further severe detriment of his calves.

"Where to, sir?" cried the driver.

"Anywhere you like!" yelled Tape, and off the taxi started, beating the policeman by a bare five yards.

The drive was such as neither Michael nor the driver (nor even possibly the bird) was ever afterwards likely to forget. First of all the gallant diplomat had his feathered companion to reckon with, and the latter was in an excessively obstreperous mood. It flapped at Tape's face with its wings; it prodded him violently in the stomach; and all the time it gave vent to blood-curdling noises which made the taxi-driver shudder, attracted the attention of all passers-by, and caused every policeman on the route to draw out his pocket-book and make a note of the number of the car. At last, however, the confounded bird appeared to tire, and had a quiet spell which gave its captor a chance to collect his thoughts.

This, of course, brought him face to face with his

second problem—where was he to take the pelican, and how was he to extract from it the precious report? Michael Tape thought and thought, and at last he came to the conclusion that the unfortunate bird would have to be killed and cut open. But who should do it? He firmly refused to face the possibility that he himself should kill the bird. It seemed rather a poulterer's job. Then he reflected again that perhaps pelicans were not poultry and that he ought to apply to a veterinary surgeon for assistance. But he knew no vet., he considered, and then the solution struck him. The greater must comprise the less! What a veterinary could do a doctor must certainly also be able to perform—and he had, among his personal friends, a distinguished surgeon who would surely come to his rescue.

"Drive to 65 Harley Street," he shouted through the speaking-tube, and the driver, relieved at being given so respectable an address, nodded assent.

Five minutes more brought him to 65 Harley Street, the house of George Redman, one of the most eminent of the younger surgeons and an old friend of Tape's. Getting out of the taxi, and slamming the door quickly before the pelican could follow him, he was about to ring the bell when the front door of the house opened and out walked a pompous gentleman whom he recognized as his Grace the Duke of Dumpshire, with whom he occasionally played bridge at his club. The Duke stared hard at Tape's muddied and dishevelled appearance, but he nodded affably enough and was about to speak to him when he suddenly noticed the pelican looking out of the taxi window.

"Heavens!" exclaimed the Duke, and he stumped off down the street, obviously under the impression that the young diplomatist (diplomatists are still young at forty) had taken leave of his senses.

Fortunately Redman was disengaged, and Tape was soon in his consulting-room, pouring out his woes to him.

"But," said the surgeon, "where do I come in?"

"Well, you see," replied Tape, "I thought you might cut the bird open for me, and recover Travers's report."

"The devil you did!" exclaimed Redman. "My dear chap, I can't operate on a pelican."

"Why not? You're a surgeon, aren't you?"

"Of course I am."

"Well, then," said Tape, "there you are! If you can cut open human beings, surely you can manage a mere bird. Why, I don't make such an awful mess, myself, of carving a chicken!"

"Anyhow," answered Redman decisively, "I'm not going to."

Tape, however, was not to be put off even with so definite a refusal. "My dear Redman," he continued, "think of the service you will be rendering to the country! Travers's report is of immense value. It may make the difference between peace and war. And then think of the good turn you will be doing to me, one of your oldest pals! For if I lose that report, it means the sack for me from the Diplomatic Office."

"And you jolly well deserve it!" was Redman's reply. Then he went on, more favourably: "But I suppose that I shall have to try to get you out of your scrape. Yet I don't fancy that it will be necessary to cut open the wretched pelican—for whom, honestly, I feel more sorry than I do for you, old chap!"

"But what else will recover the report?"

"Why, you juggins," said Redman, "have you never heard of an emetic?"

"Lord! What an idea!" shouted Tape, and before Redman could say another word he had dashed out, paid off the taxi (at the promised treble rate), and was staggering back into the house grasping once more in his arms the fluttering squawking pelican.

"Hi! Stop! Not in here, you fool!" yelled the surgeon—but too late. The pelican was already in the consulting-room, where it proceeded to flutter madly round, upsetting the telephone, the inkpot, a couple of vases of flowers and other trifles.

On the scene that followed a veil must be drawn. The reader, if he has any imagination, can reconstruct it for himself, if he chooses (which he may not). It is sufficient to say that in three-quarters of an hour that priceless envelope was recovered, but looking much the worse for its experience, and smelling amazingly of partly-digested fish. The pelican, also, was hardly looking in its best form, and the state of the consulting-room was not a credit to Harley Street.

"My dear Redman," cried Tape exultingly, when it was all over, "you can't imagine how grateful I am to you. You have saved my reputation and my position. You have quite possibly also saved England from a war. Thank you a million times, my dear fellow. Now I must get back to the

Diplomatic Office. Trumpington will be expecting me."

He made for the door, but Redman grabbed him by the arm.

"Stop a minute," said the surgeon, "what about your feathered friend here?"

Tape looked puzzled.

"Perhaps," he hesitated, "you wouldn't mind my leaving him here for a bit? I would . . ."

"No you don't, my boy," Redman assured him. "When you leave here that bird does too."

"But I can't take a pelican to the Diplomatic Office!"

"That's your trouble, not mine. After all, you stole the pelican!"

Then it was that Michael Tape's dream came to him again. He saw his chance of rounding off the adventure in a manner at once dashing and whimsical. At last there would be one of those little labels, with "Presented by Michael Tape, Esq., F.Z.S." upon it, in Regent's Park. He would present the pelican to the Zoo!

This was, of course, sheer madness—a direct result, he afterwards believed, of satanic temptation, and it led him into still more trouble. But for the moment his soul was serene and joyful. His eyes glistened.

"All right," he said, with assumed carelessness. "I'll take the beastly bird and get rid of it somehow."

Once more the poor pelican, now scarcely resisting at all, for it felt uncommonly limp after the doctoring its insides had been given, was hustled into a taxi along with Michael Tape. Soon they reached the

Zoological Society's offices, and Michael alighted and entered the building.

"I was wondering," he said to the clerk, "whether the Society would like to accept a pelican—a fine specimen—as a gift from me!"

"I should imagine, sir," replied the clerk, "that the Society would be most grateful. Perhaps you would care to write to the Secretary about it?"

"I should rather see him now," answered Tape, "for, as a matter of fact, I've got it outside in a taxi."

The clerk looked at him queerly, for he had just seen an evening paper which gave a highly coloured account of the theft that morning of one of the pelicans in St James's Park. He noticed also that Tape's clothes were muddy and that he looked as if he had been struggling with something.

"Very good, sir," said the clerk, "I will see if I can find the Secretary. Perhaps you wouldn't mind stepping into the waiting-room for a few minutes, sir?"

The unsuspecting Tape—who had forgotten all about evening papers—did as he was bid, and no sooner was he safely in, than the astute clerk telephoned to the police.

Unfortunate Michael Tape! In but a few minutes there arrived two stalwart constables who, when he tried to explain who he was, merely warned him that anything he said might be used in evidence against him, and, when he protested the excellence of his motives, answered: "All right, Mr Pelican-Pincher, you can tell them that at the station!" So to the police station he was forced to go, and only with the greatest difficulty was he able to persuade

the inspector to allow him to telephone to Sir
Charles Trumpington. Having done that he felt a
trifle easier in mind, for his chief had promised to
come round at once to see what could be done. But
Tape had to wait Sir Charles's arrival in the cells,
which he felt was no highly dignified position for a
rising light of the Diplomatic Office. He consoled
himself, however, with the thought that he had at
least got rid of the pelican, and that he had Travers's
report safe in his pocket.

Sir Charles Trumpington was as good as his word,
and before long had bailed out our hero and had
heard his story.

"I must say, Tape," he said, as they drove towards
Whitehall together, "that after your first inexcusable
carelessness in allowing that ridiculous bird to get
hold of Travers's letter, you showed commendable
perseverance in retrieving your blunder."

Tape murmured some acknowledgment of the
compliment.

"You may be amused to learn," continued Sir
Charles, "that this somewhat soiled and fishy
envelope which I hold in my hand—really I hope
you will not lose any more documents inside pelicans
—does *not* contain Travers's report."

"Doesn't contain Travers's report!" cried Tape.
"What do you mean, sir?"

"That my original calculation was correct. The
report will only arrive on Wednesday, for I have just
had a cable from Travers that he has posted it from
Brindisi to-day. This," he continued, opening the
famous envelope, "contains, let me see—only a few
Zenobian postage stamps for my grand-daughter,

Margaret. Travers is always so thoughtful. He loves to do little kindnesses of this sort when his duties take him abroad."

Then it was that Michael Tape broke into a commentary upon recent events couched in language that was not only undiplomatic, but positively unparliamentary. Sir Charles, however, took no notice, for he was, after all, not totally devoid of human sympathy.

I. A. WILLIAMS—*The Man who Stole the Pelican.*

THE LOATHLY OPPOSITE

BURMINSTER had been to a Guildhall dinner the night before, which had been attended by many —to him—unfamiliar celebrities. He had seen for the first time in the flesh people whom he had long known by reputation, and he declared that in every case the picture he had formed of them had been cruelly shattered. An eminent poet, he said, had looked like a starting-price bookmaker, and a financier of world-wide fame had been exactly like the music-master at his preparatory school. Wherefore Burminster made the profound deduction that things were never what they seemed.

"That's only because you have a feeble imagination," said Sandy Arbuthnot. "If you had really understood Timson's poetry you would have realised that it went with close-cropped red hair and a fat body, and you should have known that Macintyre (this was the financier) had the music-and-metaphysics type of mind. That's why he puzzles the City so. If you understand a man's work well enough you can guess pretty accurately what he'll look like. I don't mean the colour of his eyes and his hair, but the general atmosphere of him."

It was Sandy's agreeable habit to fling an occasional paradox at the table with the view of starting an argument. This time he stirred up Pugh, who had come to the War Office from the

Indian Staff Corps. Pugh had been a great figure in Secret Service work in the East, but he did not look the part, for he had the air of a polo-playing cavalry subaltern. The skin was stretched as tight over his cheek-bones as over the knuckles of a clenched fist, and was so dark that it had the appearance of beaten bronze. He had black hair, rather beady black eyes, and the hooky nose which in the Celt often goes with that colouring. He was himself a very good refutation of Sandy's theory.

"I don't agree," Pugh said. "At least not as a general principle. One piece of humanity whose work I studied with the microscope for two aching years upset all my notions when I came to meet it."

Then he told us this story.

"When I was brought to England in November '17 and given a 'hush' department on three floors of an eighteenth-century house in a back street, I had a good deal to learn about my business. That I learned it in reasonable time was due to the extraordinarily fine staff that I found provided for me. Not one of them was a regular soldier. They were all educated men—they had to be in that job—but they came out of every sort of environment. One of the best was a Shetland laird, another was an Admiralty Court K.C., and I had besides a metallurgical chemist, a golf champion, a leader-writer, a popular dramatist, several actuaries, and an East-end curate. None of them thought of anything but his job, and at the end of the War, when some ass proposed to make them O.B.E.'s, there was a fair imitation of a riot. A more loyal crowd never existed, and they accepted me as their chief as unquestioningly as if I had been with them since 1914.

"To the War in the ordinary sense they scarcely gave a thought. You found the same thing in a lot of other behind-the-lines departments, and I daresay it was a good thing—it kept their nerves quiet and their minds concentrated. After all our business was only to decode and decypher German messages; we had nothing to do with the use which was made of them. It was a curious little nest, and when the Armistice came my people were flabbergasted—they hadn't realised that their job was bound up with the War.

"The one who most interested me was my second-in-command, Philip Channell. He was a man of forty-three, about five-foot-four in height, weighing, I fancy, under nine stone, and almost as blind as an owl. He was good enough at papers with his double glasses, but he could hardly recognize you three yards off. He had been a professor at some Midland college—mathematics or physics, I think—and as soon as the War began he had tried to enlist. Of course they wouldn't have him—he was about E5 in any physical classification, besides being well over age—but he would take no refusal, and presently he worried his way into the Government service. Fortunately he found a job which he could do superlatively well, for I do not believe there was a man alive with more natural genius for cryptography.

"I don't know if any of you have ever given your mind to that heart-breaking subject. Anyhow

you know that secret writing falls under two heads—
codes and cyphers, and that codes are combinations
of words and cyphers of numerals. I remember
how one used to be told that no code or cypher
which was practically useful was really undiscover-
able, and in a sense that is true, especially of codes.
A system of communication which is in constant use
must obviously not be too intricate, and a working
code, if you get long enough for the job, can generally
be read. That is why a code is periodically changed
by the users. There are rules in worrying out the
permutations and combinations of letters in most
codes, for human ingenuity seems to run in certain
channels, and a man who has been a long time at the
business gets surprisingly clever at it. You begin by
finding out a little bit, and then empirically building
up the rules of de-coding, till in a week or two you
get the whole thing. Then, when you are happily
engaged in reading enemy messages, the code is
changed suddenly, and you have to start again from
the beginning. . . . You can make a code, of course,
that it is simply impossible to read except by accident
—the key to which is a page of some book, for
example—but fortunately that kind is not of much
general use.

"Well, we got on pretty well with the codes,
and read the intercepted enemy messages, cables
and wireless, with considerable ease and precision.
It was mostly diplomatic stuff, and not very important. The more valuable stuff was in cypher,
and that was another pair of shoes. With a code
you can build up the interpretation by degrees,
but with a cypher you either know it or you don't—

there are no half-way houses. A cypher, since it deals with numbers, is a horrible field for mathematical ingenuity. Once you have written out the letters of a message in numerals there are many means by which you can lock it and double-lock it. The two main devices, as you know, are transposition and substitution, and there is no limit to the ways one or other or both can be used. There is nothing to prevent a cypher having a double meaning, produced by two different methods, and, as a practical question, you have to decide which meaning is intended. By way of an extra complication, too, the message, when de-cyphered, may turn out to be itself in a difficult code. I can tell you our job wasn't exactly a rest cure."

Burminster, looking puzzled, inquired as to the locking of cyphers.

"It would take too long to explain. Roughly, you write out a message horizontally in numerals; then you pour it into vertical columns, the number and order of which are determined by a keyword; then you write out the contents of the columns horizontally, following the lines across. To unlock it you have to have the key word, so as to put it back into the vertical columns, and then into the original horizontal form."

Burminster cried out like one in pain. "It can't be done. Don't tell me that any human brain could solve such an acrostic."

"It was frequently done," said Pugh.

"By you?"

"Lord bless you, not by me. I can't do a simple cross-word puzzle. By my people."

"Give me the trenches," said Burminster in a hollow voice. "Give me the trenches any day. Do you seriously mean to tell me that you could sit down before a muddle of numbers and travel back the way they had been muddled to an original that made sense?"

"I couldn't, but Channell could—in most cases. You see, we didn't begin entirely in the dark. We already knew the kind of intricacies that the enemy favoured, and the way we worked was by trying a variety of clues till we lit on the right one."

"Well, I'm blessed! Go on about your man Channell."

"This isn't Channell's story," said Pugh. "He only comes into it accidentally. . . . There was one cypher which always defeated us, a cypher used between the German General Staff and their forces in the East. It was a locked cypher, and Channell had given more time to it than to any dozen of the others, for it put him on his mettle. But he confessed himself absolutely beaten. He wouldn't admit that it was insoluble, but he declared that he would need a bit of real luck to solve it. I asked him what kind of luck, and he said a mistake and a repetition. That, he said, might give him a chance of establishing equations.

"We called this particular cypher 'P.Y.,' and we hated it poisonously. We felt like pygmies battering at the base of a high stone tower. Dislike of the thing soon became dislike of the man who had conceived it. Channell and I used to— I won't say amuse, for it was too dashed serious

—but torment ourselves by trying to picture the
fellow who owned the brain that was responsible
for P.Y. We had a pretty complete *dossier* of the
German Intelligence Staff, but of course we couldn't
know who was responsible for this particular cypher.
We knew no more than his code name, Reinmar,
with which he signed the simpler messages to the
East, and Channell, who was a romantic little chap
for all his science, had got it into his head that it was
a woman. He used to describe her to me as if he
had seen her—a she-devil, young, beautiful, with a
much-painted white face, and eyes like a cobra's.
I fancy he read a rather low class of novel in his
off-time.

"My picture was different. At first I thought
of the histrionic type of scientist, the 'ruthless
brain' type, with a high forehead and a jaw puck-
ered like a chimpanzee. But that didn't seem
to work, and I settled on a picture of a first-
class *Generalstaboffizier*, as handsome as Falkenhayn,
trained to the last decimal, absolutely passionless,
with a mind that worked with the relentless precision of a fine machine. We all of us at the time
suffered from the bogy of this kind of German,
and, when things were going badly, as in March
'18, I couldn't sleep for hating him. The infernal
fellow was so water-tight and armour-plated, a
Goliath who scorned the pebbles from our feeble
slings.

"Well, to make a long story short, there came
a moment in September '18 when P.Y. was about
the most important thing in the world. It mattered enormously what Germany was doing in

Syria, and we knew that it was all in P.Y. Every morning a pile of the intercepted German wireless messages lay on Channell's table, which were as meaningless to him as a child's scrawl. I was prodded by my chiefs and in turn I prodded Channell. We had a week to find the key to the cypher, after which things must go on without us, and if we had failed to make anything of it in eighteen months of quiet work, it didn't seem likely that we would succeed in seven feverish days. Channell nearly went off his head with overwork and anxiety. I used to visit his dingy little room and find him fairly grizzled and shrunken with fatigue.

"This isn't a story about him, though there is a good story which I may tell you another time. As a matter of fact we won on the post. P.Y. made a mistake. One morning we got a long message dated *en clair*, then a very short message, and then a third message almost the same as the first. The second must mean 'Your message of to-day's date unintelligible please repeat,' the regular formula. This gave us a translation of a bit of the cypher. Even that would not have brought it out, and for twelve hours Channell was on the verge of lunacy, till it occurred to him that Reinmar might have signed the long message with his name, as we used to do sometimes in cases of extreme urgency. He was right, and, within three hours of the last moment Operations could give us, we had the whole thing pat. As I have said, that is a story worth telling, but it is not this one.

"We both finished the War too tired to think of much except that the darned thing was over.

But Reinmar had been so long our unseen but constantly pictured opponent that we kept up a certain interest in him. We would like to have seen how he took the licking, for he must have known that we had licked him. Mostly when you lick a man at a game you rather like him, but I didn't like Reinmar. In fact I made him a sort of compost of everything I had ever disliked in a German. Channell stuck to his she-devil theory, but I was pretty certain that he was a youngish man with an intellectual arrogance which his country's *débâcle* would in no way lessen. He would never acknowledge defeat. It was highly improbable that I should ever find out who he was, but I felt that if I did, and met him face to face, my dislike would be abundantly justified.

"As you know, for a year or two after the Armistice I was a pretty sick man. Most of us were. We hadn't the fillip of getting back to civilized comforts, like the men in the trenches. We had always been comfortable enough in body, but our minds were fagged out, and there is no easy cure for that. My digestion went nobly to pieces, and I endured a miserable space of lying in bed and living on milk and olive-oil. After that I went back to work, but the darned thing always returned, and every leech had a different regime to advise. I tried them all— dry meals, a snack every two hours, lemon juice, sour milk, starvation, knocking off tobacco—but nothing got me more than half-way out of the trough. I was a burden to myself and a nuisance to others, dragging my wing through life, with a constant pain in my tummy.

"More than one doctor advised an operation, but I was chary about that, for I had seen several of my friends operated on for the same mischief and left as sick as before. Then a man told me about a German fellow called Christoph, who was said to be very good at handling my trouble. The best hand at diagnosis in the world, my informant said—no fads—treated every case on its merits—a really original mind. Dr Christoph had a modest kurhaus at a place called Rosensee in the Sächischen Sweitz. By this time I was getting pretty desperate, so I packed a bag and set off for Rosensee.

"It was a quiet little town at the mouth of a narrow valley, tucked in under wooded hills, a clean fresh place with open channels of running water in the streets. There was a big church with an onion spire, a Catholic seminary, and a small tanning industry. The kurhaus was half-way up a hill, and I felt better as soon as I saw my bedroom, with its bare scrubbed floors and its wide verandah looking up into a forest glade. I felt still better when I saw Dr Christoph. He was a small man with a grizzled beard, a high forehead, and a limp, rather like what I imagine the Apostle Paul must have been. He looked wise, as wise as an old owl. His English was atrocious, but even when he found that I talked German fairly well he didn't expand in speech. He would deliver no opinion of any kind until he had had me at least a week under observation; but somehow I felt comforted, for I concluded that a first-class brain had got to work on me.

"The other patients were mostly Germans with a sprinkling of Spaniards, but to my delight I found Channell. He also had been having a thin time since we parted. Nerves were his trouble—general nervous debility and perpetual insomnia, and his college had given him six months' leave of absence to try to get well. The poor chap was as lean as a sparrow, and he had the large dull eyes and the dry lips of the sleepless. He had arrived a week before me, and like me was under observation. But his vetting was different from mine, for he was a mental case, and Dr Christoph used to devote hours to trying to unriddle his nervous tangles. 'He is a good man for a German,' said Channell, ' but he is on the wrong tack. There's nothing wrong with my mind. I wish he'd stick to violet rays and massage, instead of asking me silly questions about my great-grandmother.'

"Channell and I used to go for invalidish walks in the woods, and we naturally talked about the years we had worked together. He was living mainly in the past, for the War had been the great thing in his life, and his professorial duties seemed trivial by comparison. As we tramped among the withered bracken and heather his mind was always harking back to the dingy little room where he had smoked cheap cigarettes and worked fourteen hours out of the twenty-four. In particular he was as eagerly curious about our old antagonist, Reinmar, as he had been in 1918. He was more positive than ever that she was a woman, and I believe that one of the reasons that had induced him to try a cure in Germany was a vague hope that he might get on her track. I had almost forgotten about the thing, and I was amused by Channell in the part of the untiring sleuth-hound.

"'You won't find her in the Kurhaus,' I said. 'Perhaps she is in some old schloss in the neighbourhood, waiting for you like the Sleeping Beauty.'

"'I'm serious,' he said plaintively. 'It is purely a matter of intellectual curiosity, but I confess I would give a great deal to see her face to face. After I leave here, I thought of going to Berlin to make some inquiries. But I'm handicapped, for I know nobody and I have no credentials. Why don't you, who have a large acquaintance and far more authority, take the thing up?'

"I told him that my interest in the matter had flagged and that I wasn't keen on digging into the past, but I promised to give him a line to our Military Attaché if he thought of going to Berlin. I rather discouraged him from letting his mind dwell too much on events in the War. I said that he ought to try to bolt the door on all that had contributed to his present breakdown.

"'That is not Dr Christoph's opinion,' he said emphatically. 'He encourages me to talk about it. You see, with me it is a purely intellectual interest. I have no emotion in the matter. I feel quite friendly towards Reinmar, whoever she may be. It is, if you like, a piece of romance. I haven't had so many romantic events in my life that I want to forget this.'

"'Have you told Dr Christoph about Reinmar?' I asked.

"'Yes,' he said, 'and he was mildly interested.

You know the way he looks at you with his solemn grey eyes. I doubt if he quite understood what I meant, for a little provincial doctor, even though he is a genius in his own line, is not likely to know much about the ways of the Great General Staff. . . . I had to tell him, for I have to tell him all my dreams, and lately I have taken to dreaming about Reinmar.'

"'What's she like?' I asked.

"'Oh, a most remarkable figure. Very beautiful, but uncanny. She has long fair hair down to her knees.'

"Of course I laughed. 'You're mixing her up with the Valkyries,' I said. 'Lord, it would be an awkward business if you met that she-dragon in the flesh.'

"But he was quite solemn about it, and declared that his waking picture of her was not in the least like his dreams. He rather agreed with my nonsense about the old schloss. He thought that she was probably some penniless grandee, living solitary in a moated grange, with nothing now to exercise her marvellous brain on, and eating her heart out with regret and shame. He drew so attractive a character of her that I began to think that Channell was in love with a being of his own creation, till he ended with, 'But all the same she's utterly damnable. She must be, you know.'

"After a fortnight I began to feel a different man. Dr Christoph thought that he had got on the track of the mischief, and certainly, with his deep massage and a few simple drugs, I had more internal comfort than I had known for three years. He was so

pleased with my progress that he refused to treat me
as an invalid. He encouraged me to take long walks
into the hills, and presently he arranged for me to go
out roebuck-shooting with some of the local junkers.

"I used to start before daybreak on the chilly
November mornings and drive to the top of one
of the ridges, where I would meet a collection of
sportsmen and beaters, shepherded by a fellow in a
green uniform. We lined out along the ridge, and
the beaters, assisted by a marvellous collection of
dogs, including the sporting dachshund, drove the
roe towards us. It wasn't very cleverly managed,
for the deer generally broke back, and it was chilly
waiting in the first hours with a powdering of snow
on the ground and the fir boughs heavy with frost
crystals. But later, when the sun grew stronger, it
was a very pleasant mode of spending a day. There
was not much of a bag, but whenever a roe or a
capercailzie fell all the guns would assemble and drink
little glasses of *kirschwasser*. I had been lent a rifle,
one of those appalling contraptions which are
double-barrelled shot-guns and rifles in one, and to
transpose from one form to the other requires a
mathematical calculation. The rifle had a hair
trigger too, and when I first used it I was nearly
the death of a respectable Saxon peasant.

"We all ate our midday meal together and in
the evening, before going home, we had coffee
and cakes in one or other of the farms. The
party was an odd mixture, big farmers and small
squires, an hotel-keeper or two, a local doctor, and
a couple of lawyers from the town. At first they
were a little shy of me, but presently they thawed,

and after the first day we were good friends. They spoke quite frankly about the War, in which every one of them had had a share, and with a great deal of dignity and good sense.

"I learned to walk in Sikkim, and the little Saxon hills seemed to me inconsiderable. But they were too much for most of the guns, and instead of going straight up or down a slope they always chose a circuit, which gave them an easy gradient. One evening, when we were separating as usual, the beaters taking a short cut and the guns a circuit, I felt that I wanted exercise, so I raced the beaters downhill, beat them soundly, and had the better part of an hour to wait for my companions, before we adjourned to the farm for refreshment. The beaters must have talked about my pace, for as we walked away one of the guns, a lawyer called Meissen, asked me why I was visiting Rosensee at a time of year when few foreigners came. I said I was staying with Dr Christoph.

"'Is he then a private friend of yours?' he asked.

"I told him No, that I had come to his kurhaus for treatment, being sick. His eyes expressed polite scepticism. He was not prepared to regard as an invalid a man who went down a hill like an avalanche.

"But, as we walked in the frosty dusk, he was led to speak of Dr Christoph, of whom he had no personal knowledge, and I learned how little honour a prophet may have in his own country. Rosensee scarcely knew him, except as a doctor who had an inexplicable attraction for foreign patients. Meissen was curious about his methods and the exact diseases in which he specialized. 'Perhaps he may yet save me a journey to Homburg?' he laughed. 'It is well to have a skilled physician at one's doorstep. The doctor is something of a hermit, and except for his patients does not appear to welcome his kind. Yet he is a good man, beyond doubt, and there are those who say that in the War he was a hero.'

"This surprised me, for I could not imagine Dr Christoph in any fighting capacity, apart from the fact that he must have been too old. I thought that Meissen might refer to work in the base hospitals. But he was positive; Dr Christoph had been in the trenches; the limping leg was a war wound.

"I had had very little talk with the doctor, owing to my case being free from nervous complications. He would say a word to me morning and evening about my diet, and pass the time of day when we met, but it was not till the very eve of my departure that we had anything like a real conversation. He sent a message that he wanted to see me for not less than one hour, and he arrived with a batch of notes from which he delivered a kind of lecture on my case. Then I realized what an immense amount of care and solid thought he had expended on me. He had decided that his diagnosis was right—my rapid improvement suggested that—but it was necessary for some time to observe a simple regime, and to keep an eye on certain symptoms. So he took a sheet of note-paper from the table and in his small precise hand wrote down for me a few plain commandments.

"There was something about him, the honest eyes, the mouth which looked as if it had been often compressed in suffering, the air of grave good-will, which I found curiously attractive. I wished that I had been a mental case like Channell, and had had more of his society. I detained him in talk, and he seemed not unwilling. By and by we drifted to the War and it turned out that Meissen was right.

"Dr Christoph had gone as medical officer in November '14 to the Ypres Salient with a Saxon regiment, and had spent the winter there. In '15 he had been in Champagne, and in the early months of '16 at Verdun, till he was invalided with rheumatic fever. That is to say, he had had about seventeen months of consecutive fighting in the worst areas with scarcely a holiday. A pretty good record for a frail little middle-aged man!

"His family was then at Stuttgart, his wife and one little boy. He took a long time to recover from the fever, and after that was put on home duty. 'Till the War was almost over,' he said, 'almost over, but not quite. There was just time for me to go back to the front and get my foolish leg hurt.' I must tell you that whenever he mentioned his war experience it was with a comical deprecating smile, as if he agreed with anyone who might think that gravity like his should have remained in bed.

"I assumed that this home duty was medical, until he said something about getting rusty in his professional work. Then it appeared that it had been some job connected with Intelligence. 'I

am reputed to have a little talent for mathematics,'
he said. 'No. I am no mathematical scholar,
but, if you understand me, I have a certain mathematical aptitude. My mind has always moved
happily among numbers. Therefore I was set to
construct and to interpret cyphers, a strange inter-
lude in the noise of war. I sat in a little room
and excluded the world, and for a little I was happy.'

"He went on to speak of the *enclave* of peace
in which he had found himself, and as I listened
to his gentle monotonous voice, I had a sudden
inspiration.

"I took a sheet of note-paper from the stand,
scribbled the word *Reinmar* on it, and shoved it
towards him. I had a notion, you see, that I
might surprise him into helping Channell's researches.

"But it was I who got the big surprise. He
stopped thunderstruck, as soon as his eye caught
the word, blushed scarlet over every inch of face
and bald forehead, seemed to have difficulty in
swallowing, and then gasped. 'How did you
know?'

"I hadn't known, and now that I did, the knowledge left me speechless. This was the loathly
opposite for which Channell and I had nursed our
hatred. When I came out of my stupefaction I
found that he had recovered his balance and was
speaking slowly and distinctly, as if he were making a
formal confession.

"'You were among my opponents . . . that
interests me deeply. . . . I often wondered. . . .
You beat me in the end. You are aware of that?'

"I nodded. 'Only because you made a slip,' I said.

"'Yes, I made a slip. I was to blame—very gravely to blame, for I let my private grief cloud my mind.'

"He seemed to hesitate, as if he were loath to stir something very tragic in his memory.

"'I think I will tell you,'" he said at last. 'I have often wished—it is a childish wish—to justify my failure to those who profited by it. My chiefs understood, of course, but my opponents could not. In that month when I failed I was in deep sorrow. I had a little son—his name was Reinmar—you remember that I took that name for my code signature?'

"His eyes were looking beyond me into some vision of the past.

"'He was, as you say, my mascot. He was all my family, and I adored him. But in those days food was not plentiful. We were no worse off than many million Germans, but the child was frail. In the last summer of the War he developed phthisis due to malnutrition, and in September he died. Then I failed my country, for with him some virtue seemed to depart from my mind. You see, my work was, so to speak, his also, as my name was his, and when he left me he took my power with him. . . . So I stumbled. The rest is known to you.'

"He sat staring beyond me, so small and lonely, that I could have howled. I remember putting my hand on his shoulder, and stammering some platitude about being sorry. We sat quite still for a minute or two, and then I remembered Channell. Channell must have poured his views of Reinmar into Dr Christoph's ear. I asked him if Channell knew.

A flicker of a smile crossed his face.

"'Indeed no. And I will exact from you a promise never to breathe to him what I have told you. He is my patient, and I must first consider his case. At present he thinks that Reinmar is a wicked and beautiful lady whom he may some day meet. That is romance, and it is good for him to think so. . . . If he were told the truth, he would be pitiful, and in Herr Channell's condition it is important that he should not be vexed with such emotions as pity.'"

JOHN BUCHAN—*The Runagates Club*.

THE STALLED OX

THEOPHIL ESHLEY was an artist by profession, a cattle painter by force of environment. It is not to be supposed that he lived on a ranch or a dairy farm, in an atmosphere pervaded with horn and hoof, milking-stool, and branding-iron. His home was in a park-like, villa-dotted district that only just escaped the reproach of being suburban. On one side of his garden there abutted a small, picturesque meadow, in which an enterprising neighbour pastured some small picturesque cows of the Channel Island persuasion. At noonday in summertime the cows stood knee-deep in tall meadow-grass under the shade of a group of walnut trees, with the sunlight falling in dappled patches on their mouse-sleek coats. Eshley had conceived and executed a dainty picture of two reposeful milch-cows in a setting of walnut-tree and meadow-grass and filtered sunbeam, and the Royal Academy had duly exposed the same on the walls of its Summer Exhibition. The Royal Academy encourages orderly, methodical habits in its children. Eshley had painted a successful and acceptable picture of cattle drowsing picturesquely under walnut trees, and as he had begun, so, of necessity, he went on. His "Noontide Peace," a study of two dun cows under a walnut tree, was followed by "A Mid-day Sanctuary," a study of a walnut tree, with two dun cows under it. In due succession there came "Where the Gad-Flies Cease from Troubling," "The Haven of the Herd," and "A Dream in Dairyland," studies of walnut trees and dun cows. His two attempts to break away from his own tradition were signal failures: "Turtle Doves alarmed by Sparrow-hawk" and "Wolves on the Roman Campagna" came back to his studio in the guise of abominable heresies, and Eshley climbed back into grace and the public gaze with "A Shaded Nook where Drowsy Milkers Dream."

On a fine afternoon in late autumn he was putting some finishing touches to a study of meadow weeds when his neighbour, Adela Pingsford, assailed the outer door of his studio with loud peremptory knockings.

"There is an ox in my garden," she announced, in explanation of the tempestuous intrusion.

"An ox," said Eshley blankly, and rather fatuously; "what kind of ox?"

"Oh, I don't know what kind," snapped the lady. "A common or garden ox, to use the slang expression. It is the garden part of it that I object to. My garden has just been put straight for the winter, and an ox roaming about in it won't improve matters. Besides, there are the chrysanthemums just coming into flower."

"How did it get into the garden?" asked Eshley.

"I imagine it came in by the gate," said the lady impatiently; "it couldn't have climbed the walls, and I don't suppose anyone dropped it from an aeroplane as a Bovril advertisement. The immediately important question is not how it got in, but how to get it out."

"Won't it go?" said Eshley.

"If it was anxious to go," said Adela Pingsford rather angrily, "I should not have come here to chat with you about it. I'm practically all alone; the housemaid is having her afternoon out and the cook is lying down with an attack of neuralgia. Anything that I may have learned at school or in after life about how to remove a large ox from a small garden seems to have escaped from my memory now. All I could think of was that you were a near neighbour and a cattle painter, presumably more or less familiar with the subjects that you painted, and that you might be of some slight assistance. Possibly I was mistaken."

"I paint dairy cows, certainly," admitted Eshley, "but I cannot claim to have had any experience in rounding up stray oxen. I've seen it done on a cinema film, of course, but there were always horses and lots of other accessories; besides, one never knows how much of those pictures are faked."

Adela Pingsford said nothing, but led the way to her garden. It was normally a fair-sized garden, but it looked small in comparison with the ox, a huge mottled brute, dull red about the head and shoulders, passing to dirty white on the flanks and hind-quarters, with shaggy ears and large blood-shot eyes. It bore about as much resemblance to the dainty paddock heifers that Eshley was accustomed to paint as the chief of a Kurdish nomad clan would to a Japanese tea-shop girl. Eshley stood very near the gate while he studied the animal's appearance and demeanour. Adela Pingsford continued to say nothing.

"It's eating a chrysanthemum," said Eshley at last, when the silence had become unbearable.

"How observant you are," said Adela bitterly. "You seem to notice everything. As a matter of fact, it has got six chrysanthemums in its mouth at the present moment."

The necessity for doing something was becoming imperative. Eshley took a step or two in the direction of the animal, clapped his hands, and made noises of the "Hish" and "Shoo" variety. If the ox heard them it gave no outward indication of the fact.

"If any hens should ever stray into my garden," said Adela, "I should certainly send for you to frighten them out. You 'shoo' beautifully. Meanwhile, do you mind trying to drive that ox away? That is a *Mademoiselle Louise Bichot* that he's begun on now," she added in icy calm, as a glowing orange head was crushed into the huge munching mouth.

"Since you have been so frank about the variety of the chrysanthemum," said Eshley, "I don't mind telling you that this is an Ayrshire ox."

The icy calm broke down; Adela Pingsford used language that sent the artist instinctively a few feet nearer to the ox. He picked up a pea-stick and flung it with some determination against the animal's mottled flanks. The operation of mashing *Mademoiselle Louise Bichot* into a petal salad was suspended for a long moment, while the ox gazed with concentrated inquiry at the stick-thrower. Adela gazed with equal concentration and more obvious hostility at the same focus. As the beast neither lowered its head nor stamped its feet Eshley

ventured on another javelin exercise with another
pea-stick. The ox seemed to realize at once that it
was to go; it gave a hurried final pluck at the bed
where the chrysanthemums had been, and strode
swiftly up the garden. Eshley ran to head it towards
the gate, but only succeeded in quickening its pace
from a walk to a lumbering trot. With an air of
inquiry, but with no real hesitation, it crossed the
tiny strip of turf that the charitable called the
croquet lawn, and pushed its way through the open
French window into the morning-room. Some
chrysanthemums and other autumn herbage stood
about the room in vases, and the animal resumed its
browsing operations; all the same, Eshley fancied
that the beginnings of a hunted look had come into
its eyes, a look that counselled respect. He dis-
continued his attempt to interfere with its choice of
surroundings.

"Mr Eshley," said Adela in a shaking voice, "I
asked you to drive that beast out of my garden, but
I did not ask you to drive it into my house. If I
must have it anywhere on the premises I prefer the
garden to the morning-room."

"Cattle drives are not in my line," said Eshley;
"if I remember I told you so at the outset."

"I quite agree," retorted the lady, "painting
pretty pictures of pretty little cows is what you're
suited for. Perhaps you'd like to do a nice sketch
of that ox making itself at home in my morning-
room?"

This time it seemed as if the worm had turned;
Eshley began striding away.

"Where are you going?" screamed Adela.

"To fetch implements," was the answer.

"Implements? I won't have you use a lasso. The room will be wrecked if there's a struggle."

But the artist marched out of the garden. In a couple of minutes he returned, laden with easel, sketching-stool, and painting materials.

"Do you mean to say that you're going to sit quietly down and paint that brute while it's destroying my morning-room?" gasped Adela.

"It was your suggestion," said Eshley, setting his canvas in position.

"I forbid it; I absolutely forbid it!" stormed Adela.

"I don't see what standing you have in the matter," said the artist; "you can hardly pretend that it's your ox, even by adoption."

"You seem to forget that it's in my morning-room, eating my flowers," came the raging retort.

"You seem to forget that the cook has neuralgia," said Eshley; "she may be just dozing off into a merciful sleep and your outcry will waken her. Consideration for others should be the guiding principle of people in our station of life."

"The man is mad!" exclaimed Adela tragically. A moment later it was Adela herself who appeared to go mad. The ox had finished the vase-flowers and the cover of "Israel Kalisch," and appeared to be thinking of leaving its rather restricted quarters. Eshley noticed its restlessness and promptly flung it some bunches of Virginia creeper leaves as an inducement to continue the sitting.

"I forget how the proverb runs," he observed; "something about 'better a dinner of herbs than a

stalled ox where hate is.' We seem to have all the
ingredients for the proverb ready to hand."

"I shall go to the Public Library and get them to
telephone for the police," announced Adela, and,
raging audibly, she departed.

Some minutes later the ox, awakening probably
to the suspicion that oil cake and chopped mangold
was waiting for it in some appointed byre, stepped
with much precaution out of the morning-room,
stared with grave inquiry at the no longer obtrusive
and pea-stick-throwing human, and then lumbered
heavily but swiftly out of the garden. Eshley packed
up his tools and followed the animal's example and
"Larkdene" was left to neuralgia and the cook.

The episode was the turning-point in Eshley's
artistic career. His remarkable picture, "Ox in a
morning-room, late autumn," was one of the sensa-
tions and successes of the next Paris Salon, and when
it was subsequently exhibited at Munich it was
bought by the Bavarian Government, in the teeth of
the spirited bidding of three meat-extract firms.
From that moment his success was continuous and
assured, and the Royal Academy was thankful, two
years later, to give a conspicuous position on its walls
to his large canvas "Barbary Apes Wrecking a
Boudoir."

Eshley presented Adela Pingsford with a new copy
of "Israel Kalisch," and a couple of finely flowering
plants of *Madame André Blusset*, but nothing in the
nature of a real reconciliation has taken place
between them.

SAKI—*Beasts and Super-beasts.*

QUALITY

I KNEW him from the days of my extreme youth, because he made my father's boots; inhabiting with his elder brother two little shops let into one, in a small by-street—now no more, but then most fashionably placed in the West End.

That tenement had a certain quiet distinction; there was no sign upon its face that he made for any of the Royal Family—merely his own German name of Gessler Brothers; and in the window a few pairs of boots. I remember that it always troubled me to account for those unvarying boots in the window, for he made only what was ordered, reaching nothing down, and it seemed so inconceivable that what he made could ever have failed to fit. Had he bought them to put there? That, too, seemed inconceivable. He would never have tolerated in his house leather on which he had not worked himself. Besides, they were too beautiful— the pair of pumps, so inexpressibly slim, the patent leathers with cloth tops, making water come into one's mouth, the tall brown riding-boots with marvellous sooty glow, as if, though new, they had been worn a hundred years. Those pairs could only have been made by one who saw before him the Soul of Boot—so truly were they prototypes incarnating the very spirit of all footgear. These thoughts, of course, came to me later, though even when I was promoted to him, at the age of perhaps fourteen, some inkling haunted me of the dignity of himself and brother. For to make boots—such boots as he made—seemed to me then, and still seems to me, mysterious and wonderful.

I remember well my shy remark, one day, while stretching out to him my youthful foot:

"Isn't it awfully hard to do, Mr Gessler?"

And his answer, given with a sudden smile from out of the sardonic redness of his beard: "Id is an Ardt!"

Himself, he was a little as if made from leather, with his yellow crinkly face, and crinkly reddish hair and beard, and neat folds slanting down his cheeks to the corners of his mouth, and his guttural and one-toned voice; for leather is a sardonic substance, and stiff and slow of purpose. And that was the character of his face, save that his eyes, which were grey-blue, had in them the simple gravity of one secretly possessed by the Ideal. His elder brother was so very like him—though watery, paler in every way, with a great industry—that sometimes in early days I was not quite sure of him until the interview was over. Then I knew that it was he, if the words, "I will ask my brudder," had not been spoken; and that, if they had, it was his elder brother.

When one grew old and wild and ran up bills, one somehow never ran them up with Gessler Brothers. It would not have seemed becoming to go in there and stretch out one's foot to that blue iron-spectacled glance, owing him for more than—say—two pairs, just the comfortable reassurance that one was still his client.

For it was not possible to go to him very often—his boots lasted terribly, having something beyond the temporary—some, as it were, essence of boot stitched into them.

One went in, not as into most shops, in the mood of: "Please serve me, and let me go!" but restfully, as one enters a church; and, sitting on the single wooden chair, waited—for there was never anybody there. Soon, over the top edge of that sort of well—rather dark, and smelling soothingly of leather—which formed the shop, there would be seen his face, or that of his elder brother, peering down. A guttural sound, and the tip-tap of bast slippers beating the narrow wooden stairs, and he would stand before one without coat, a little bent, in leather apron, with sleeves turned back, blinking—as if awakened from some dream of boots, or like an owl suprised in daylight and annoyed at this interruption.

And I would say: "How do you do, Mr Gessler? Could you make me a pair of Russia leather boots?"

Without a word he would leave me, retiring whence he came, or into the other portion of the shop, and I would continue to rest in the wooden chair, inhaling the incense of his trade. Soon he would come back, holding in his thin, veined hand a piece of gold-brown leather. With eyes fixed on it, he would remark: "What a beaudiful biece!" When I, too, had admired it, he would speak again. "When do you wand dem?" And I would answer: "Oh! As soon as you conveniently can." And he would say: "To-morrow fordnighd?" Or if he were his elder brother: "I will ask my brudder!"

Then I would murmur: "Thank you! Good-morning, Mr Gessler." "Goot-morning!" he would reply, still looking at the leather in his hand. And as I moved to the door, I would hear the tip-tap of his bast slippers restoring him, up the stairs, to his dream of boots. But if it were some new kind of footgear that he had not yet made me, then indeed he would observe ceremony—divesting me of my boot and holding it long in his hand, looking at it with eyes at once critical and loving, as if recalling the glow with which he had created it, and rebuking the way in which one had disorganized this master-piece. Then, placing my foot on a piece of paper, he would two or three times tickle the outer edges with a pencil and pass his nervous fingers over my toes, feeling himself into the heart of my require-ments.

I cannot forget that day on which I had occasion to say to him: "Mr Gessler, the last pair of town walking-boots creaked, you know."

He looked at me for a time without replying, as if expecting me to withdraw or qualify the state-ment, then said:

"Id shouldn'd 'ave greaked."

"It did, I'm afraid."

"You goddem wed before dey found demselves?"

"I don't think so."

At that he lowered his eyes, as if hunting for memory of those boots, and I felt sorry I had mentioned this grave thing.

"Zend dem back!" he said; "I will look at dem."

A feeling of compassion for my creaking boots

surged up in me, so well could I imagine the sorrow-ful long curiosity of regard which he would bend on them.

"Zome boods," he said slowly, "are bad from birdt. If I can do noding wid dem, I dake dem off your bill."

Once (once only) I went absent-mindedly into his shop in a pair of boots bought in an emergency at some large firm's. He took my order without showing me any leather, and I could feel his eyes penetrating the inferior integument of my foot. At last he said:

"Dose are nod my boods."

The tone was not one of anger, nor of sorrow, not even of contempt, but there was in it some-thing quiet that froze the blood. He put his hand down and pressed a finger on the place where the left boot, endeavouring to be fashionable, was not quite comfortable.

"Id 'urds you dere," he said. "Dose big virms 'ave no self-respect. Drash!" And then, as if something had given way within him, he spoke long and bitterly. It was the only time I ever heard him discuss the conditions and hardships of his trade.

"Dey get id all," he said, "dey get id by adverdise-ment, nod by work. Dey dake it away from us, who lofe our boods. Id gomes to this—bresently I haf no work. Every year id gets less—you will see." And looking at his lined face I saw things I had never noticed before, bitter things and bitter struggle—and what a lot of grey hairs there seemed suddenly in his red beard!

As best I could, I explained the circumstances of the purchase of those ill-omened boots. But his face and voice made a so deep impression that during the next few minutes I ordered many pairs. Nemesis fell! They lasted more terribly than ever. And I was not able conscientiously to go to him for nearly two years.

When at last I went I was surprised to find that outside one of the two little windows of his shop another name was painted, also that of a boot-maker—making, of course, for the Royal Family. The old familiar boots, no longer in dignified isolation, were huddled in the single window. Inside, the now contracted well of the one little shop was more scented and darker than ever. And it was longer than usual, too, before a face peered down, and the tip-tap of the bast slippers began. At last he stood before me, and, gazing through those rusty iron spectacles, said:

"Mr ——, isn'd id?"

"Ah! Mr Gessler," I stammered, "but your boots are really *too* good, you know! See, these are quite decent still!" And I stretched out to him my foot. He looked at it.

"Yes," he said, "beople do nod wand good boods, id seems."

To get away from his reproachful eyes and voice I hastily remarked: "What have you done to your shop?"

He answered quietly: "Id was too exbensif. Do you wand some boods?"

I ordered three pairs, though I had only wanted two, and quickly left. I had I know not quite what feeling of being part, in his mind, of a conspiracy against him; or not perhaps so much against him as against his idea of boot. One does not, I suppose, care to feel like that; for it was again many months before my next visit to his shop, paid, I remember, with the feeling: "Oh! well, I can't leave the old boy—so here goes! Perhaps it'll be his elder brother!"

For his elder brother, I knew, had not character enough to reproach me, even dumbly.

And, to my relief, in the shop there did appear to be his elder brother, handling a piece of leather.

"Well, Mr Gessler," I said, "how are you?"

He came close, and peered at me.

"I am breddy well," he said slowly; "but my elder brudder is dead."

And I saw that it was indeed himself—but how aged and wan! And never before had I heard him mention his brother. Much shocked, I murmured: "Oh! I am sorry!"

"Yes," he answered, "he was a good man, he made a good bood; but he is dead." And he touched the top of his head, where the hair had suddenly gone as thin as it had been on that of his poor brother, to indicate, I suppose, the cause of death. "He could nod ged over losing de oder shop. Do you wand any boods?" And he held up the leather in his hand: "Id's a beaudiful biece."

I ordered several pairs. It was very long before they came—but they were better than ever. One simply could not wear them out. And soon after that I went abroad.

It was over a year before I was again in London. And the first shop I went to was my old friend's. I had left a man of sixty, I came back to one of seventy-five, pinched and worn and tremulous, who genuinely, this time, did not at first know me.

"Oh! Mr Gessler," I said, sick at heart; "how splendid your boots are! See, I've been wearing this pair nearly all the time I've been abroad; and they're not halfworn out, are they?"

He looked long at my boots—a pair of Russia leather, and his face seemed to regain steadiness. Putting his hand on my instep, he said:

"Do dey vid you here? I 'ad drouble wid dat bair, I remember."

I assured him that they had fitted beautifully.

"Do you wand any boods?" he said. "I can make dem quickly; id is a slack dime."

I answered: "Please, please! I want boots all round—every kind!"

"I will make a vresh model. Your food must be bigger." And with utter slowness, he traced round my foot, and felt my toes, only once looking up to say:

"Did I dell you my brudder was dead?"

To watch him was painful, so feeble had he grown; I was glad to get away.

I had given those boots up, when one evening they came. Opening the parcel, I set the four pairs out in a row. Then one by one I tried them on. There was no doubt about it. In shape and fit, in finish and quality of leather, they were the best he had ever made me. And in the mouth of one of the town walking-boots I found his bill.

The amount was the same as usual, but it gave me quite a shock. He had never before sent it in till quarter day. I flew downstairs and wrote a cheque, and posted it at once with my own hand.

A week later, passing the little street, I thought I would go in and tell him how splendidly the new boots fitted. But when I came to where his shop had been, his name was gone. Still there, in the window, were the slim pumps, the patent leathers with cloth tops, the sooty riding-boots.

I went in, very much disturbed. In the two little shops—again made into one—was a young man with an English face.

"Mr Gessler in?" I said.

He gave me a strange, ingratiating look.

"No, sir," he said, "no. But we can attend to anything with pleasure. We've taken the shop over. You've seen our name, no doubt, next door. We make for some very good people."

"Yes, yes," I said; but Mr Gessler?"

"Oh!" he answered; "dead."

"Dead! But I only received these boots from him last Wednesday week."

"Ah!" he said; "a shockin' go. Poor old man starved 'imself."

"Good God!"

"Slow starvation, the doctor called it! You see he went to work in such a way! Would keep the shop on; wouldn't have a soul touch his boots except himself. When he got an order, it took him such a time. People won't wait. He lost everybody. And there he'd sit, goin' on and on—I will say that for him—not a man in London made a better boot! But look at the competition! He never advertised! Would 'ave the best leather, too, and do it all 'imself. Well, there it is. What could you expect with his ideas?"

"But starvation——!"

"That may be a bit flowery, as the sayin' is—but I know myself he was sittin' over his boots day and night, to the very last. You see I used to watch him. Never gave 'imself time to eat; never had a penny in the house. All went in rent and leather. How he lived so long I don't know. He regular let his fire go out. He was a character. But he made good boots."

"Yes," I said, "he made good boots."

JOHN GALSWORTHY—*Selected Short Stories.*

THE COP AND THE ANTHEM

On his bench in Madison Square Soapy moved uneasily. When wild goose honk high of nights, and when women without sealskin coats grow kind to their husbands, and when Soapy moves uneasily on his bench in the park, you may know that winter is near at hand.

A dead leaf fell in Soapy's lap. That was Jack Frost's card. Jack is kind to the regular denizens of Madison Square, and gives fair warning of his annual call. At the corners of four streets he hands his pasteboard to the North Wind, footman of the mansion of All Outdoors, so that the inhabitants thereof may make ready.

Soapy's mind became cognizant of the fact that the time had come for him to resolve himself into a singular Committee of Ways and Means to provide against the coming rigour. And therefore he moved uneasily on his bench.

The hibernatorial ambitions of Soapy were not of the highest. In them there were no considerations of Mediterranean cruises, of soporific Southern skies or drifting in the Vesuvian Bay. Three months on the Island was what his soul craved. Three months of assured board and bed and congenial company, safe from Boreas and bluecoats, seemed to Soapy the essence of things desirable.

For years the hospitable Blackwell's had been his

winter quarters. Just as his more fortunate fellow
New Yorkers had bought their tickets to Palm
Beach and the Riviera each winter, so Soapy had
made his humble arrangements for his annual hegira
to the Island. And now the time was come. On
the previous night three Sabbath newspapers, distrib-
uted beneath his coat, about his ankles and over his
lap, had failed to repulse the cold as he slept on his
bench near the spurting fountain in the ancient
square. So the Island loomed large and timely in
Soapy's mind. He scorned the provisions made in
the name of charity for the city's dependents. In
Soapy's opinion the Law was more benign than
Philanthropy. There was an endless round of in-
stitutions, municipal and eleemosynary, on which he
might set out and receive lodging and food accordant
with the simple life. But to one of Soapy's proud
spirit the gifts of charity are encumbered. If not
in coin you must pay in humiliation of spirit for
every benefit received at the hands of philanthropy.
As Cæsar had his Brutus, every bed of charity must
have its toll of a bath, every loaf of bread its com-
pensation of a private and personal inquisition.
Wherefore it is better to be a guest of the law, which,
though conducted by rules, does not meddle unduly
with a gentleman's private affairs.

Soapy, having decided to go to the Island, at once
set about accomplishing his desire. There were
many easy ways of doing this. The pleasantest was
to dine luxuriously at some expensive restaurant; and
then, after declaring insolvency, be handed over
quietly and without uproar to a policeman. An
accommodating magistrate would do the rest.

Soapy left his bench and strolled out of the square and across the level sea of asphalt, where Broadway and Fifth Avenue flow together. Up Broadway he turned, and halted at a glittering café, where are gathered together nightly the choicest products of the grape, the silkworm and the protoplasm.

Soapy had confidence in himself from the lowest button of his vest upward. He was shaven, and his coat was decent and his neat black, ready-tied four-in-hand had been presented to him by a lady missionary on Thanksgiving Day. If he could reach a table in the restaurant unsuspected success would be his. The portion of him that would show above the table would raise no doubt in the waiter's mind. A roasted mallard duck, thought Soapy, would be about the thing—with a bottle of Chablis, and then Camembert, a demi-tasse and a cigar. One dollar for the cigar would be enough. The total would not be so high as to call forth any supreme manifestation of revenge from the café management; and yet the meat would leave him filled and happy for the journey to his winter refuge.

But as Soapy set foot inside the restaurant door the head waiter's eye fell upon his frayed trousers and decadent shoes. Strong and ready hands turned him about and conveyed him in silence and haste to the sidewalk and averted the ignoble fate of the menaced mallard.

Soapy turned off Broadway. It seemed that his route to the coveted Island was not to be an epicurean one. Some other way of entering limbo must be thought of.

At a corner of Sixth Avenue electric lights and

cunningly displayed wares behind plate-glass made a shop window conspicuous. Soapy took a cobble-stone and dashed it through the glass. People came running round the corner, a policeman in the lead. Soapy stood still, with his hands in his pockets, and smiled at the sight of brass buttons.

"Where's the man that done that?" inquired the officer excitedly.

"Don't you figure out that I might have had something to do with it?" said Soapy, not without sarcasm, but friendly, as one greets good fortune.

The policeman's mind refused to accept Soapy even as a clue. Men who smash windows do not remain to parley with the law's minions. They take to their heels. The policeman saw a man half-way down the block running to catch a car. With drawn club he joined in the pursuit. Soapy, with disgust in his heart, loafed along, twice unsuccessful.

On the opposite side of the street was a restaurant of no great pretensions. It catered to large appetites and modest purses. Its crockery and atmosphere were thick; its soup and napery thin. Into this place Soapy took his accusive shoes and tell-tale trousers without challenge. At a table he sat and consumed beefsteak, flapjacks, doughnuts and pie. And then to the waiter he betrayed the fact that the minutest coin and himself were strangers.

"Now, get busy and call a cop," said Soapy. "And don't keep a gentleman waiting."

"No cop for youse," said the waiter, with a voice like butter cakes and an eye like the cherry in a Manhattan cocktail. "Hey, Con!"

Neatly upon his left ear on the callous pavement two waiters pitched Soapy. He arose, joint by joint, as a carpenter's rule opens, and beat the dust from his clothes. Arrest seemed but a rosy dream. The Island seemed very far away. A policeman who stood before a drug store two doors away laughed and walked down the street.

Five blocks Soapy travelled before his courage permitted him to woo capture again. This time the opportunity presented what he fatuously termed to himself a "cinch." A young woman of a modest and pleasing guise was standing before a show window gazing with sprightly interest at its display of shaving mugs and inkstands, and two yards from the window a large policeman of severe demeanour leaned against a water-plug.

It was Soapy's design to assume the rôle of the despicable and execrated "masher." The refined and elegant appearance of his victim and the contiguity of the conscientious cop encouraged him to believe that he would soon feel the pleasant official clutch upon his arm that would ensure his winter quarters on the right little, tight little isle.

Soapy straightened the lady missionary's ready-made tie, dragged his shrinking cuffs into the open, set his hat at a killing cant and sidled toward the young woman. He made eyes at her, was taken with sudden coughs and "hems," smiled, smirked and went brazenly through the impudent and contemptible litany of the "masher." With half an eye Soapy saw that the policeman was watching him fixedly. The young woman moved away a few steps, and again bestowed her absorbed attention upon the shaving mugs. Soapy followed, boldly stepping to her side, raised his hat and said:

"Ah there, Bedelia! Don't you want to come and play in my yard?"

The policeman was still looking. The persecuted young woman had but to beckon a finger and Soapy would be practically *en route* for his insular haven. Already he imagined he could feel the cosy warmth of the station-house. The young woman faced him and, stretching out a hand, caught Soapy's coat-sleeve.

"Sure, Mike," she said joyfully, "if you'll blow me to a pail of suds. I'd have spoke to you sooner, but the cop was watching."

With the young woman playing the clinging ivy to his oak Soapy walked past the policeman, over-come with gloom. He seemed doomed to liberty.

At the next corner he shook off his companion and ran. He halted in the district where by night are found the lightest streets, hearts, vows and librettos. Women in furs and men in greatcoats moved gaily in the wintry air. A sudden fear seized Soapy that some dreadful enchantment had rendered him immune to arrest. The thought brought a little of panic upon it, and when he came upon another policeman lounging grandly in front of a trans-plendent theatre he caught at the immediate straw of "disorderly conduct."

On the sidewalk Soapy began to yell drunken gibberish at the top of his harsh voice. He danced, howled, raved and otherwise disturbed the welkin.

The policeman twirled his club, turned his back to Soapy and remarked to a citizen:

"'Tis one of them Yale lads celebratin' the goose egg they give to the Hartford College. Noisy; but no harm. We've instructions to lave them be."

Disconsolate, Soapy ceased his unavailing racket. Would never a policeman lay hands on him? In his fancy the Island seemed an unattainable Arcadia. He buttoned his thin coat against the chilling wind.

In a cigar store he saw a well-dressed man lighting a cigar at a swinging light. His silk umbrella he had set by the door on entering. Soapy stepped inside, secured the umbrella and sauntered off with it slowly. The man at the cigar light followed hastily.

"My umbrella," he said sternly.

"Oh, is it?" sneered Soapy, adding insult to petit larceny. "Well, why don't you call a policeman? I took it. Your umbrella! Why don't you call a cop? There stands one at the corner."

The umbrella owner slowed his steps. Soapy did likewise, with a presentiment that luck would again run against him. The policeman looked at the two curiously.

"Of course," said the umbrella man—"that is— well, you know how these mistakes occur—I—if it's your umbrella I hope you'll excuse me—I picked it up this morning in a restaurant—if you recognize it as yours, why—I hope you'll——"

"Of course it's mine," said Soapy viciously.

The ex-umbrella man retreated. The policeman hurried to assist a tall blonde in an opera cloak across the street in front of a street car that was approaching two blocks away.

Soapy walked eastward through a street damaged

by improvements. He hurled the umbrella wrath-
fully into an excavation. He muttered against the
men who wear helmets and carry clubs. Because he
wanted to fall into their clutches, they seemed to
regard him as a king who could do no wrong.

At length Soapy reached one of the avenues to the
east where the glitter and turmoil was but faint. He
set his face down this toward Madison Square, for
the homing instinct survives even when the home is a
park bench.

But on an unusually quiet corner Soapy came to a
standstill. Here was an old church, quaint and
rambling and gabled. Through one violet-stained
window a soft light glowed, where, no doubt, the
organist loitered over the keys, making sure of his
mastery of the coming Sabbath anthem. For there
drifted out to Soapy's ears sweet music that caught
and held him transfixed against the convolutions of
the iron fence.

The moon was above, lustrous and serene;
vehicles and pedestrians were few; sparrows twit-
tered sleepily in the eaves—for a little while the
scene might have been a country churchyard. And
the anthem that the organist played cemented Soapy
to the iron fence, for he had known it well in the days
when his life contained such things as mothers and
roses and ambitions and friends and immaculate
thoughts and collars.

The conjunction of Soapy's receptive state of mind
and the influences about the old church wrought a
sudden and wonderful change in his soul. He
viewed with swift horror the pit into which he had
tumbled, the degraded days, unworthy desires, dead

hopes, wrecked faculties and base motives that made up his existence.

And also in a moment his heart responded thrillingly to this novel mood. An instantaneous and strong impulse moved him to battle with his desperate fate. He would pull himself out of the mire; he would make a man of himself again; he would conquer the evil that had taken possession of him. There was time; he was comparatively young yet; he would resurrect his old eager ambitions and pursue them without faltering. Those solemn but sweet organ notes had set up a revolution in him. To-morrow he would go into the roaring down-town district and find work. A fur importer had once offered him a place as driver. He would find him to-morrow and ask for the position. He would be somebody in the world. He would——

Soapy felt a hand laid on his arm. He looked quickly around into the broad face of a policeman.

"What are you doin' here?" asked the officer.

"Nothin'," said Soapy.

"Then come along," said the policeman.

"Three months on the Island," said the Magistrate in the Police Court the next morning.

O. HENRY—*The Best of O. Henry.*

THE DIAMOND MAKER

SOME business had detained me in Chancery Lane
until nine in the evening, and thereafter, having some
inkling of a headache, I was disinclined either for
entertainment or further work. So much of the sky
as the high cliffs of that narrow cañon of traffic left
visible spoke of a serene night, and I determined to
make my way down to the Embankment, and rest
my eyes and cool my head by watching the variegated
lights upon the river. Beyond comparison the night
is the best time for this place; a merciful darkness
hides the dirt of the waters, and the lights of this
transition age, red, glaring orange, gas-yellow, and
electric white, are set in shadowy outlines of every
possible shade between grey and deep purple.
Through the arches of Waterloo Bridge a hundred
points of light mark the sweep of the Embankment,
and above its parapet rise the towers of Westminster,
warm grey against the starlight. The black river
goes by with only a rare ripple breaking its silence,
and disturbing the reflections of the lights that swim
upon its surface.

"A warm night," said a voice at my side.

I turned my head, and saw the profile of a man who
was leaning over the parapet beside me. It was a
refined face, not unhandsome, though pinched and
pale enough, and the coat collar turned up and
pinned round the throat marked his status in life as

sharply as a uniform. I felt I was committed to the price of a bed and breakfast if I answered him.

I looked at him curiously. Would he have anything to tell me worth the money, or was he the common incapable—incapable even of telling his own story? There was a quality of intelligence in his forehead and eyes, and a certain tremulousness in his nether lip that decided me.

"Very warm," said I; "but not too warm for us here."

"No," he said, still looking across the water, "it is pleasant enough here . . . just now."

"It is good," he continued after a pause, "to find anything so restful as this in London. After one has been fretting about business all day, about getting on, meeting obligations, and parrying dangers, I do not know what one would do if it were not for such pacific corners." He spoke with long pauses between the sentences. "You must know a little of the irksome labour of the world, or you would not be here. But I doubt if you can be so brain-weary and foot-sore as I am . . . Bah! Sometimes I doubt if the game is worth the candle. I feel inclined to throw the whole thing over—name, wealth, and position—and take to some modest trade. But I know if I abandoned my ambition—hardly as she uses me—I should have nothing but remorse left for the rest of my days."

He became silent. I looked at him in astonishment. If ever I saw a man hopelessly hard-up it was the man in front of me. He was ragged and he was dirty, unshaven and unkempt; he looked as though he had been left in a dust-bin for a week.

And he was talking to *me* of the irksome worries of a large business. I almost laughed outright. Either he was mad or playing a sorry jest on his own poverty.

"If high aims and high positions," said I, "have their drawbacks of hard work and anxiety, they have their compensations. Influence, the power of doing good, of assisting those weaker and poorer than ourselves; and there is even a certain gratification in display. . . . "

My banter under the circumstances was in very vile taste. I spoke on the spur of the contrast of his appearance and speech. I was sorry even while I was speaking.

He turned a haggard but very composed face upon me. Said he: "I forget myself. Of course you would not understand."

He measured me for a moment. "No doubt it is very absurd. You will not believe me even when I tell you, so that it is fairly safe to tell you. And it will be a comfort to tell someone. I really have a big business in hand, a very big business. But there are troubles just now. The fact is . . . I make diamonds."

"I suppose," said I, "you are out of work just at present?"

"I am sick of being disbelieved," he said impatiently, and suddenly unbuttoning his wretched coat he pulled out a little canvas bag that was hanging by a cord round his neck. From this he produced a brown pebble. "I wonder if you know enough to know what that is?" He handed it to me.

Now, a year or so ago, I had occupied my leisure in taking a London science degree, so that I have a smattering of physics and mineralogy. The thing was not unlike an uncut diamond of the darker sort, though far too large, being almost as big as the top of my thumb. I took it, and saw it had the form of a regular octahedron, with the carved faces peculiar to the most precious of minerals. I took out my penknife and tried to scratch it—vainly. Leaning forward towards the gas-lamp, I tried the thing on my watch-glass, and scored a white line across that with the greatest ease.

I looked at my interlocutor with rising curiosity. "It certainly is rather like a diamond. But, if so, it is a Behemoth of diamonds. Where did you get it?"

"I tell you I made it," he said. "Give it back to me."

He replaced it hastily and buttoned his jacket. "I will sell it you for one hundred pounds," he suddenly whispered eagerly. With that my suspicions returned. The thing might, after all, be merely a lump of that almost equally hard substance, corundum, with an accidental resemblance in shape to the diamond. Or if it was a diamond, how came he by it, and why should he offer it at a hundred pounds?

We looked into one another's eyes. He seemed eager, but honestly eager. At that moment I believed it was a diamond he was trying to sell. Yet I am a poor man, a hundred pounds would leave a visible gap in my fortunes and no sane man would buy a diamond by gaslight from a ragged tramp on his personal warranty only. Still, a diamond that size conjured up a vision of many thousands of pounds. Then, thought I, such a stone could scarcely exist without being mentioned in every book on gems, and again I called to mind the stories of contraband and light-fingered Kaffirs at the Cape. I put the question of purchase on one side.

"How did you get it?" said I.

"I made it."

I had heard something of Moissan, but I knew his artificial diamonds were very small. I shook my head.

"You seem to know something of this kind of thing. I will tell you a little about myself. Perhaps then you may think better of the purchase." He turned round with his back to the river, and put his hands in his pockets. He sighed. "I know you will not believe me."

"Diamonds," he began—and as he spoke his voice lost its faint flavour of the tramp and assumed something of the easy tone of an educated man— "are to be made by throwing carbon out of combination in a suitable flux and under a suitable pressure; the carbon crystallizes out, not as black-lead or charcoal-powder, but as small diamonds. So much has been known to chemists for years, but no one yet has hit upon exactly the right flux in which to melt up the carbon, or exactly the right pressure for the best results. Consequently the diamonds made by chemists are small and dark, and worthless as jewels. Now I, you know, have given up my life to this problem—given my life to it.

"I began to work at the conditions of diamond making when I was seventeen, and now I am thirty-two. It seemed to me that it might take all the thought and energies of a man for ten years, or twenty years, but, even if it did, the game was still worth the candle. Suppose one to have at last just hit the right trick, before the secret got out and diamonds became as common as coal, one might realise millions. Millions!"

He paused and looked for my sympathy. His eyes shone hungrily. "To think," said he, "that I am on the verge of it all, and here!"

"I had," he proceeded, "about a thousand pounds when I was twenty-one, and this, I thought, eked out by a little teaching, would keep my researches going. A year or two was spent in study, at Berlin chiefly, and then I continued on my own account. The trouble was the secrecy. You see, if once I had let out what I was doing, other men might have been spurred on by my belief in the practicability of the idea; and I do not pretend to be such a genius as to have been sure of coming in first, in the case of a race for the discovery. And you see it was important that if I really meant to make a pile, people should not know that it was an artificial process and capable of turning out diamonds by the ton. So I had to work all alone. At first I had a little laboratory, but as my resources began to run out I had to conduct my experiments in a wretched unfurnished room in Kentish Town, where I slept at last on a straw mattress on the floor among all my apparatus. The money simply flowed away. I grudged myself everything except scientific appliances. I tried to keep things going by a little teaching, but I am not a very good teacher, and I have no university degree, nor very much education except in chemistry, and I found I had to give a lot of time and labour for precious little money. But I got nearer and nearer the thing. Three years ago I settled the problem of the composition of the flux, and got near the pressure by putting this flux of mine and a certain carbon composition into a closed-up gun-barrel, filling up with water, sealing tightly, and heating."

He paused.

"Rather risky," said I.

"Yes. It burst, and smashed all my windows and a lot of my apparatus; but I got a kind of diamond powder nevertheless. Following out the problem of getting a big pressure upon the molten mixture from which the things were to crystallize, I hit upon some researches of Daubrée's at the Paris *Laboratorie des Poudres et Salpêtres*. He exploded dynamite in a tightly screwed steel cylinder, too strong to burst, and I found he could crush rocks into a muck not unlike the South African bed in which diamonds are found. It was a tremendous strain on my resources, but I got a steel cylinder made for my purpose after his pattern. I put in all my stuff and my explosives, built up a fire in my furnace, put the whole concern in, and—went out for a walk."

I could not help laughing at his matter-of-fact manner. "Did you not think it would blow up the house? Were there other people in the place?"

"It was in the interest of science," he said ultimately. "There was a costermonger family on the floor below, a begging-letter writer in the room behind mine, and two flower-women were upstairs. Perhaps it was a bit thoughtless. But possibly some of them were out.

"When I came back the thing was just where I left it, among the white-hot coals. The explosive hadn't burst the case. And then I had a problem to face. You know time is an important element in crystalliza-tion. If you hurry the process the crystals are small —it is only by prolonged standing that they grow to any size. I resolved to let this apparatus cool for two years, letting the temperature go down slowly during that time. And I was now quite out of money; and with a big fire and the rent of my room, as well as my hunger to satisfy, I had scarcely a penny in the world.

"I can hardly tell you all the shifts I was put to while I was making the diamonds. I have sold newspapers, held horses, opened cab-doors. For many weeks I addressed envelopes. I had a place as assistant to a man who owned a barrow, and used to call down one side of the road while he called down the other. Once for a week I had abso-lutely nothing to do, and I begged. What a week that was! One day the fire was going out and I had eaten nothing all day, and a little chap taking his girl out, gave me sixpence—to show-off. Thank heaven for vanity! How the fish-shops smelt! But I went and spent it all on coals, and had the furnace bright red again, and then—— Well, hunger makes a fool of a man.

"At last, three weeks ago, I let the fire out. I took my cylinder and unscrewed it while it was still so hot that it punished my hands, and I scraped out the crumbling lava-like mass with a chisel, and hammered it into a powder upon an iron plate. And I found three big diamonds and five small ones. As I sat on the floor hammering, my door opened, and my neighbour, the begging-letter writer, came in. He was drunk—as he usually is. ''Nerchist,' said he. 'You're drunk,' said I. ''Structive scoundrel,' said he. 'Go to your father,' said I, meaning the Father of Lies. 'Never you mind,' said he, and gave me a cunning wink, and hiccupped, and leaning up against the door, with his other eye against the door-post, began to babble of how he had been prying in my room, and how he had gone to the police that morning, and how they had taken down everything he had to say—''siffiwas a ge'm,' said he. Then I suddenly realized I was in a hole. Either I should have to tell these police my little secret, and get the whole thing blown upon, or be lagged as an anarchist. So I went up to my neighbour and took him by the collar, and rolled him about a bit, and then I gathered up my diamonds and cleared out. The evening newspapers called my den the Kentish-Town Bomb Factory. And now I cannot part with the things for love or money.

"If I go in to a respectable jewellers they ask me to wait, and go and whisper to a clerk to fetch a policeman, and then I say I cannot wait. And I found out a receiver of stolen goods, and he simply stuck to the one I gave him and told me to prosecute if I wanted it back. I am going about now with several hundred thousand pounds-worth of diamonds round my neck, and without either food or shelter. You are the first person I have taken into my confidence. But I like your face and I am hard-driven."

He looked into my eyes.

"It would be madness," said I, "for me to buy a diamond under the circumstances. Besides, I do not carry hundreds of pounds about in my pocket. Yet I more than half believe your story. I will, if you like, do this: come to my office to-morrow. . . ."

"You think I am a thief!" said he keenly. "You will tell the police. I am not coming into a trap."

"Somehow I am assured you are no thief. Here is my card. Take that, anyhow. You need not come to any appointment. Come when you will."

He took the card, and an earnest of my good-will.

"Think better of it and come," said I.

He shook his head doubtfully. "I will pay back your half-crown with interest some day—such interest as will amaze you," said he. "Anyhow, you will keep the secret? . . . Don't follow me."

He crossed the road and went into the darkness towards the little steps under the archway leading into Essex Street, and I let him go. And that was the last I ever saw of him.

Afterwards I had two letters from him asking me to send bank-notes—not cheques—to certain addresses. I weighed the matter over, and took what I conceived to be the wisest course. Once he called upon me when I was out. My urchin described him as a very thin, dirty, and ragged man, with a dreadful cough. He left no message. That was the finish of him so far as my story goes. I wonder sometimes what has become of him. Was he an ingenious monomaniac, or a fraudulent dealer in pebbles, or has he really made diamonds as he asserted? The latter is just sufficiently credible to make me think at times that I have missed the most brilliant opportunity of my life. He may of course be dead, and his diamonds carelessly thrown aside—one, I repeat, was almost as big as my thumb. Or he may be still wandering about trying to sell the things. It is just possible he may yet emerge upon society, and, passing athwart my heavens in the serene altitude sacred to the wealthy and the well-advertised, reproach me silently for my want of enterprise. I sometimes think I might at least have risked five pounds.

H. G. WELLS—*The Short Stories of.*

NOTES AND QUESTIONS

THE CARGO OF RICE

Cecil Scott Forester was born in Cairo in 1899. He spent his boyhood in a busy London suburb and attended Dulwich College. For some time he studied medicine at Guy's Hospital but gave that up for writing. He acted as a foreign correspondent for *The Times* but is chiefly known for his novels, especially the Hornblower series. At present Forester is living in California.

One type of short story that has always existed and is likely to continue to appeal is "the rattling good yarn," a narrative of interesting and exciting incident which grips us right away and holds our attention. We read on because we are keen to know what happens next. Forester is a master of this type of story.

1. The opening of a story generally introduces us to the setting, indicates the kind of action we may expect, and brings on the chief character. Discuss the first paragraph of this story and in particular the opening sentence.

2. What do we learn about the character of Hornblower from his first thoughts and actions?

3. The first crisis in this story is the discovery of the hole in the vessel's side. Describe briefly in your own words how Hornblower tackles this problem.

4. If you want to know what happens to Hornblower next read the story "The Penalty of Failure" which follows this story in *Mr Midshipman Hornblower*.

THE CONGER EEL

Liam O'Flaherty was born on the Aran Islands, County Galway, in 1896. Educated at University College, Dublin, he served in the British Army during the 1914–18 war and on the republican side in the Irish Civil War. He has travelled widely, often working his passage, and among other things he has been a porter, a clerk, a lumber-jack, a copper-miner and a dock labourer.

O'Flaherty began to write in London in 1922 but for subjects he generally turns to Ireland. His most popular novel is probably *The Informer* which has been filmed. His short stories have been collected under the title of *The Short Stories of Liam O'Flaherty* (Cape).

In his writing O'Flaherty is simple and direct but his stories are filled with imagination and feeling and a tone that can best, perhaps, be described as lyric. His stories dealing with animals are among his best writings and *The Conger Eel* is a good example of his unique gifts.

1. Note how quickly the action is introduced. How did the mackerel manage to escape?

2. You will not have come across the word *nable*. Can you guess the meaning? Why were the fishermen so frightened?

3. The effect of the story depends largely on the striking phrases and images O'Flaherty uses: "his black mysterious body glistened and twirled like a wisp in a foaming cataract." Can you find any other examples?

4. You may be interested to try another story of fishing, *The Old Man and the Sea* by Ernest

Hemingway which is admirably told. It is a long short-story. A full scale novel dealing with whale-hunting is Melville's *Moby Dick*.

THE SWEET SHOT

Edmund Clerihew Bentley was born in London in 1875 and educated at St Paul's School and Oxford. He became a journalist and author and is especially famous for an ingenious form of amusing verses called Clerihews after his middle name:

> Sir Christopher Wren,
> Said, "I'm going to dine with some men.
> If anybody calls
> Say I'm designing St Paul's."

Bentley is not a prolific writer but his *Trent's Last Case* is generally regarded as a model detective story, ingenious but not far-fetched, and a good novel as well as a good detective story. The story selected here is from the collection of short stories called *Trent Intervenes*.

1. How much do you learn from the opening paragraph?

2. Dialogue can illustrate the character of the speakers, help on the action of the story and liven up the story. Discuss the use made of dialogue in this story.

3. What is the critical clue? Prove it.

4. Write a short character-sketch of Trent based on evidence in this story.

5. If you like detection stories try some by Agatha Christie. They are cleverly contrived and brightly written.

THE VOYAGE

Katherine Mansfield Beauchamp was born in New Zealand in 1888 and educated at Queen's College, London. She married John Middleton Murry the literary critic. Throughout her short life she suffered from ill-health and she died in France at the age of thirty-four. Her short stories were collected in several volumes: *Bliss*, *The Garden Party*, and *The Doll's House*. There is a volume of *Selected Stories* in the World's Classics (Oxford).

Katherine Mansfield was undoubtedly influenced by Chekhov but she achieved a style of her own. Her method is impressionistic, her writing fresh, and her sensibility acute. In writing of children in particular she shows a fine understanding and delicate tenderness.

1. This story, as so often in Katherine Mansfield, is largely told through the eyes of a little girl. Can you mention any special phrases that illustrate this?

2. What part in the story does the stewardess play?

3. What picture do you form of Grandpa?

4. Other stories by Katherine Mansfield you may find interesting are: *The Doll's House*, *The Garden Party* and *Life of Ma Parker*.

THE BLUE BEAD

Norah Burke, daughter of R. St G. Burke, for twenty years in the Imperial Forest Service of India, now lives in England but most of her writing springs from her early experiences in India. Together with her father she is an author of *Jungle Days* a book dealing with big game hunting and camp life in India.

The story of her own life as a child in the jungles of India is told in *Jungle Child*. Norah Burke (Mrs Warlond) has written a number of short stories and in 1954 was first equal in the *New York Herald Tribune* contest for short stories. "The Blue Bead" was selected by John Pudney for appearance in his *Pick of To-day's Short Stories*, 1955.

Sibia, the little girl in this story really lived, and she remained stored in the author's brain for more than thirty years before she became the heroine of *The Blue Bead*.

1. Note how each element in the story is briefly introduced: the crocodile, the blue bead, Sibia. Where does the action first begin?

2. How could Sibia manage to give a vulnerable blow to such a huge animal?

3. The ending of a short story is very important. Read the last sentence very carefully. What is its real significance; that is, what lies behind the words of little Sibia?

4. If you have enjoyed this story try *Jungle Child* by the same author, and *The Jungle Books* by Rudyard Kipling.

FEAR

Herbert Ernest Bates was born in 1905 and attended Kettering Grammar School. He began to write early in life and a selection of his short stories has appeared entitled *Thirty One Tales*. In addition he has written a number of novels of which *Fair Stood the Wind for France* and *The Purple Plain* are among the most popular.

During the war Bates served with the R.A.F. and wrote short stories under the pseudonym of Flying Officer "X."

Bates is one of our leading writers of the short story. He has studied the form carefully and written an admirable study *The Modern Short Story*. Though keenly interested in character he does not despise plot and his best stories often suggest the effect of poetry. This story, "Fear," appeared in *The Best Short Stories of 1927*.

1. What helped the boy to overcome his fear?

2. The old man was not afraid during the thunderstorm. What made him begin to fear?

3. Do you think the title *Fear* is well chosen for this story? Why?

4. There are a number of contrasts in the story. Mention some.

THE LUNCHEON

WILLIAM SOMERSET MAUGHAM was born in 1874 and educated at King's School, Canterbury, and St Thomas's Hospital, London, where he qualified as a doctor. He did not practise, however, but became a writer and has proved very successful as a playwright, a novelist, and a short story writer. His travels in the Far East and in the South Seas provided him with much of the material for his stories which have recently been collected in three volumes.

Maugham prefers short stories that have a beginning, a middle, and an end, and a plot that is carefully constructed. It is interesting to note that several of his short stories have been filmed. Other short stories by Maugham that you may enjoy are in the Ashenden series and deal with the secret service.

1. The story is written in the first person. Do you think the story gains (or loses) in any way from this manner of telling?

2. Describe in a brief paragraph the character of the lady in the story.

3. Outline the plot in two sentences.

4. Maugham complains that the word most often applied to him is "competent." Do you consider that a good description of this story?

THE MAN WHO STOLE THE PELICAN

I. A. Williams was born at Middlesbrough in 1890 and educated at Rugby and King's College, Cambridge. He served in France in the 1914–18 war and was biographical correspondent for the *London Mercury* from 1920 to 1939. Since then he has been on the staff of *The Times*.

Williams has written poetry as well as short stories, and is keenly interested in natural history. *The Man who Stole the Pelican* appeared first in the *London Mercury*.

1. The story gains its effect in part from the seemingly-solemn tone in which it is told. Mention some phrases which illustrate this.

2. Where does the story reach its climax?

3. This kind of story usually has a twist at the end. Where does the twist come in here?

4. If you like humorous stories you might care to try some by W. W. Jacobs and some by P. G. Wodehouse.

THE LOATHLY OPPOSITE

John Buchan was born in Perth in 1875 and educated at Hutcheson's Grammar School, Glasgow, Glasgow University and Oxford. He served under Lord Milner after the South African war, was a partner in a publishing firm, Member of Parliament for the Scottish Universities, and finally Governor-General of Canada. He was raised to the peerage in 1935 as first Baron Tweedsmuir, and died in 1940.

In the 1914–18 war Buchan served as a colonel with Military Intelligence and it was while he was in hospital that he found the "thrillers" he was given to read were not very interesting, so he determined to write some himself. He produced *The Thirty-Nine Steps* in 1915, *Greenmantle* in 1916, and a succession of stories of adventure ending with *Sick Heart River* in 1941.

He also wrote a number of biographies, of which *Sir Walter Scott* and *Montrose* are perhaps the best. His autobiography, *Memory Holds the Door*, was published in 1940.

"The Loathly Opposite" appears in a book of short stories entitled *The Runagates Club*.

1. This story is in a frame or setting, a form now not very popular. Does it gain in any way by being told indirectly?

2. Where do you think the climax comes in this story?

3. How would you describe Dr Christoph's character?

4. You may like to try some of the other stories in *The Runagates Club*. Each is told by a different character.

THE STALLED OX

Hector Hugo Munro was born in Burma in 1870 and educated privately and at Bedford School. He joined the Burma police but had to resign for health reasons. Returning to England he became a journalist and wrote for the *Westminster Gazette*. He also wrote stories under the pseudonym of "Saki," the name of the cupbearer in Omar Khayyam's *Rubaiyat*. When the first Great War broke out Munro joined up, and in 1916 he was killed in action. This story comes from the volume of short stories called *Beasts and Superbeasts*.

"Saki," who had rather an unhappy childhood, often writes about children, especially naughty children. His writing sparkles with epigrams, his approach is always witty, and he springs surprises on us at most unexpected moments and always in a most urbane manner. He is never ordinary and never sentimental.

1. The opening paragraphs set the scene, introduce the characters, and lead on to the story. Show how the dialogue that follows supports points already made in the opening paragraph.

2. What picture do you form of Eshley?

3. What picture do you form of Adela?

4. "Saki" loved the bizarre, the unexpected, the topsy-turvy. Illustrate his point of view from this story.

QUALITY

John Galsworthy was born in 1867 and educated at Harrow and Oxford. He died in 1933. Galsworthy wrote novels of which *The Forsyte Saga* (containing "The

Man of Property," "In Chancery," and "To Let") is the most famous. It was very popular and was widely discussed.

Galsworthy has also written plays of which *The Silver Box*, *Strife*, and *Justice* are perhaps the best known. Galsworthy was keenly interested in social justice, in the lack of understanding between classes, and in the changing customs and standards of his day.

Pity is a word often, and rightly, applied to Galsworthy's attitude. Himself secure both financially and socially, he was keenly aware of the insecurity of many people's lives. *Quality* is a very characteristic piece of his writing.

1. This story is told in the first person. Does the story gain anything from this method of telling?

2. What sort of person is the narrator?

3. Do you consider the title appropriate? Why?

4. It might be said that this story is about a theme rather than about individuals. What is the theme?

THE COP AND THE ANTHEM

O. Henry is the pen name of William Sidney Porter who was born in North Carolina in 1862. He worked in turn in a drugstore, on a ranch, and in a bank. In his writing he specialized in the short story, turning out a vast number. A selection of them appears in an omnibus volume, *The Best of O. Henry*. O. Henry died in New York in 1910.

The author of some six hundred short stories is bound to be uneven, but at his best O. Henry is a highly diverting, warm-hearted writer, good natured, witty and skilful. He exploited the trick ending, the surprise in the last paragraph, to the full, generally with great success. Sometimes, it is true, the effect seems too contrived. Sometimes, too, this warm human sentiment slips over into sentimentality, but not when he is at his best. Although his popularity is now waning a little, it is likely that a few of his best stories will continue to survive.

1. This story illustrates the conciseness of a good short story where nothing is introduced which is not essential. Give the outline of the plot in not more than five short sentences.

2. The story contains a number of warm human touches. Can you give any examples?

3. O. Henry is often praised for the skilful openings of his stories. Comment on the opening of *The Cop and the Anthem*.

4. Did the ending take you by surprise? Re-read the story and note how the ending is led up to.

THE DIAMOND MAKER

Herbert George Wells was born in Kent in 1866 and was an apprentice draper, and a teacher in Midhurst Grammar School before he graduated from the Normal School of Science, South Kensington. His early life is reflected in *Mr Polly* and *Kipps*. He wrote scientific romances such as *The Time Machine*, *The Invisible Man* and *The War of the Worlds*, and novels full of social criticism of which *Tono Bungay* is perhaps his best. *The Shape of Things to Come* (1933) describes the world of 2160 A.D. as Wells imagines it will be, and *Experiment in Autobiography* (1934) reveals frankly the story of his own life. Wells died in London in 1946.

As a short story writer Wells is in the first rank. He was bubbling over with imagination and could describe the most fantastic happenings with an air of reality. Although he tended to be careless about style in his larger works, Wells exercises great economy of words in his short stories, and his phrases are often not merely sharp and compact but also vivid and illuminating.

"The Diamond Maker" is a good example of his special type of scientific fantasy. It appeared in a collection called *The Stolen Bacillus*.

1. What picture do you form of the character of the narrator?

2. Does the stranger's story seem to you credible or do you think he is an imposter? Give your reasons.

3. If you like this story, try some others by Wells. Among his best are *The Country of the Blind, The Magic Shop, The Truth about Pyecraft, The Beautiful Suit* and *The Star*.

GENERAL QUESTIONS

1. Mention two stories which, in your opinion, are well constructed. Give evidence.

2. Select two stories which, in your opinion, show good characterization, and describe the main characters in each briefly in your own words.

3. Mention two stories which depend for their effect on a surprise ending. How is this effected?

4. Mention one story which is remarkable, in your opinion, for its "atmosphere." How has the writer achieved this effect?

5. Which story have you found most amusing? Recommend it to a friend in a letter and say why you think he will enjoy it.

6. Which story, in your opinion, would make the best film? Give reasons.

7. A story should have a good title. Pick two titles which you consider as very good and two which you consider as less good. Give reasons.

8. Which story, in your opinion, has the best opening? Give reasons.

9. Which story, in your opinion, has the best ending? Give reasons.

10. Which story has appealed to you least? State your reasons.

11. Having read all the stories in this book attempt a definition of the short story: say what elements you regard as essential in the short story and point out what distinguishes the short story from the novel and from the literary sketch.

12. And now, why not try to write a short story of your own? It can be based on school-life, adventure, science, or anything that has started off your imagination. Keep it short and make sure it has a " point."